I0719682

Broken Vessel
AN URBAN SUSPENSE
A Novel
By Empress

A Novel By Empress

Broken Vessel

An Urban Suspense

A Novel By
Empress

Pearly Gates Publishing LLC
INSPIRING CHRISTIAN AUTHORS TO BE AUTHORS

Pearly Gates Publishing, LLC, Houston, Texas

Broken Vessel

Broken Vessel
An Urban Suspense

Copyright © 2018
Empress

All Rights Reserved.
No portion of this publication may be reproduced, stored in any
electronic system, or transmitted in any form or by any means
(electronic, mechanical, photocopy, recording, or otherwise) without
written permission from the author or publisher. Brief quotations
may be used in literary reviews.

This is a work of fiction. Names, businesses, places, events, locales,
and incidents are either the products of the author's imagination or
used in a fictitious manner. Any resemblance to actual persons,
living or dead, or actual events is purely coincidental.

ISBN 13: 978-1-947445-36-9
Library of Congress Control Number: 2018958293

Printed in the United States of America.

For information and bulk ordering, contact:
Pearly Gates Publishing, LLC
Angela R. Edwards, CEO
P.O. Box 62287
Houston, TX 77205
BestSeller@PearlyGatesPublishing.com

DEDICATION

I would like to dedicate this book to my Creator,
my Heavenly Father.
Without Him, this would be impossible.

ACKNOWLEDGMENTS

First, I would like to thank my **Heavenly Father**, The Lord Almighty Himself, for blessing me with the gift of writing and for giving me this vision It wasn't easy, but it was worth it. He sat me down and placed me in a situation where He was able to gain my attention, which enabled me to focus on what was ahead of me

To my sister and best friend, **Sonia**: I love you so much. Thank you for always having my back, supporting me in everything that I do, and not giving up on me. I thank God for the bond that we share, but most of all, I thank you for being my inspiration. You are a great mother, friend, and an aspiring friend.

A special thank you to my mother, **Ann Marie Johnson**, for being the woman you are today. Thank you for being my backbone and for all the advice you have given me over the years. Thank you, Mom, for all your support, never giving up on me, and always having my back—no matter what the consequences may be. You are such a blessing to me, and I am proud to be your daughter. As I grow older each day, I admire how you always seem to achieve the impossible. I might not say it every day, but I am thankful for everything you have done for me. I love you!

A special thank you for my father, **Constantine Hall**, for all you've done for me. You are the definition of a real father. You never turned your back on me and even when I was wrong, in your eyes, I was right. Daddy, thank you for all your support and the wisdom you have taught me. It's truly amazing how God placed you in my life as my father, but you're so much more. You're my friend, protector, role-dawg, and my whole heart.

To anyone else I didn't mention, I sincerely apologize. Nonetheless, I would like to thank you all for the roles you have played in my life and for any encouragement you've given me.

A LETTER FROM THE AUTHOR

Dear Readers,

I am proud to say I am honored to be one of God's chosen vessels. He has blessed me with all the right words to turn this story into a book.

I can boldly say that the person I was five years ago is not the same person I am today. It wasn't easy getting to where I am now, but it was well worth it. Through the trials and tribulations, the Lord has always been by my side, holding my hand, and carrying me through life's toughest times. Every brick that has been thrown at me I've used to firmly stand on because I believed God at His Word when He promised me that 'No weapon formed against me shall prosper."

For many, this may not seem like a big deal, but for me, this is a closed door to my past and opened doors to my future that's filled with nothing but blessings and great opportunities.

I encourage all of you to think of life's journey as a trip. Consider where you're going and what you nccd to gct there. Believe in yourself but most of all, believe in The One who has given us life.

Wherever you are today, I would like to say to you that no matter what you're going through, He is able to carry you through. Take your eyes off what's seen before you and choose to walk by faith because He is the Author and Finisher of our faith.

~ Empress ~

PREFACE

You're not the message; you're just His messenger. So, if you seriously think that GOD can't use you, well, you should think again because:

- ➢ Abraham was too old.
- ➢ Jacob lied.
- ➢ Leah was too ugly.
- ➢ Joseph was betrayed by his brothers.
- ➢ Moses stuttered.
- ➢ Gideon was afraid.
- ➢ The Samaritan woman had multiple husbands.
- ➢ Samson was a womanizer.
- ➢ Noah was an alcoholic.
- ➢ Rahab was a prostitute.
- ➢ David was a murderer and adulterer.
- ➢ The disciples fell asleep while Jesus was praying.
- ➢ Elijah was suicidal.
- ➢ Isaiah preached while he was naked.
- ➢ Jonah was stubborn and ran from GOD.
- ➢ Naomi was a widow and angry at GOD.
- ➢ Job lost everything he once owned, including his children.
- ➢ Peter denied Jesus Christ three times.
- ➢ Martha worried about everything.
- ➢ Paul was a murderer of Christians.

Everyone who has done a great work for the LORD was once a sinner. He doesn't see the mess that you are; He uses the mess that people see and turns that into a message for HIS glory. Your past doesn't determine your future.

Jeremiah 29:11 says, *"For I know the plans I have for you,"* declares the LORD, *"plans to prosper you and not to harm you, plans to give you hope and a future."*

Broken Vessel

TABLE OF CONTENTS

A Novel By Empress

Chapter 1: Kelis
Normal? What's That?

BOOM! BOOM! BOOM! Shanece opened the door. BOOM! BOOM! "Nece, you heard me. I'm not playing with you. I said you better open up the door before I…"

"Before you what? Huh? I can't hear you. Before you do what? Yeah, that's what I thought 'cause you ain't gon do a damn thing."

Those were the last words I heard my mother say as she yanked the door open and then slammed it hard, causing the pictures hanging on the wall to hit the floor. Within minutes, I overheard them yelling at each other and loud noises stemming from their bedroom. They were fighting again, going at each other's throats like two pit bulls in a pen.

My father, Mr. Curtis Jones, is the Bishop at The First Baptist Church of Christ and, of course, none other than my mother, Shanece Jones, is the First Lady—and when I say "First Lady," that's exactly what I mean. She wears that title very well for people who don't know her. Ever since my sister, Raven, and I were toddlers, this has been an ongoing ritual between my parents. Mother would begin her weekends every Friday night, right after Bible study. Then, come Sunday morning, she'd be up and ready in her Sunday's best.

"Kelis, what's on your mind?" Raven asked, interrupting the crazy thoughts that never seemed to fade away.

"I was kinda wondering what we're doing this year for Christmas," I replied. I faced the wall, listening to the continuous sounds that will never get old, no matter how old we get.

Our mother had given birth to identical twins on Christmas. I'll never forget the story she told us…

She was buck wild and running the streets when she met our father. Like most people, having kids wasn't part of the plans she once envisioned for her life. Having kids would have put a stop to her "chasing the bag." When she got the news that she was pregnant, she was four months along and at the abortion clinic ready to abort us— until the doctor gave her the horrifying news that she was pregnant with twins. She often reminded us that we should be grateful because if it weren't for each other, we wouldn't be here. Well, those were her exact words until about three years ago when she called herself getting saved, sanctified, and filled with the Holy Spirit.

It was awfully quiet in the house except for the unknown objects that were being tossed around between my parents and the ruckus of their constant arguing.

"Nece, now you need to stop this foolishness. Enough is enough. You can't continue to behave this way. One minute, you wanna act like the perfect wife; the next, you wanna allow the devil to use you," my father reasoned.

"Look at the pot calling the kettle black!"

Daddy must have struck a nerve because the noise grew louder. They continued verbally attacking each other about whose sins were greater and called each other hypocrites.

Facing Raven, I told her, "Maybe we should spend Christmas at grandpa's house." I waited for a response but never received one. Instead, she looked at me harshly, rolled her eyes, and turned her head in the opposite direction. Before I drifted off to sleep, I spent hours listening to the drama and imagining what a normal life would feel like.

Chapter 2: Kelis
Bishop, Practice What YOU Preach!

I was grateful that it was Sunday. That meant for the remainder of the week, between school and soccer practice, we would be busy and away from the nonsense that always seemed to find its way into our home. This morning was no different, though, as I sat in the pew and witnessed as our mother—wearing her Givenchy dress—took her rightful position as the First Lady. Daddy, who was no better, stood at the pulpit addressing the congregation about sins.

"Saints, the Bible says if you repent from your sins, He—the Lord—is faithful and just to forgive you. Now, when I say to repent, that doesn't mean that you simply say, "Hey, God: You and I both know that I did this and that and yeah, I know I was dead wrong. I'm simply asking You to forgive me." Now, don't get me wrong. Only He knows your heart. I'm not saying if you tell it to Him straight like that, He won't forgive you. What I'm saying to you is that when I say to repent, that doesn't mean you ask GOD for forgiveness and five minutes later go back and do the same thing. To repent means to turn from, to set aside the things that are causing you to sin such as lust, greed, jealousy, pride, and adultery. Do you need me to say it one more time?" Daddy then paused and looked around at the entire congregation. He then rested his eyes on our mother for what seemed like forever. Feeling guilty, she fidgeted and acted as if she was removing lint from her dress. Wiping his face, he continued. "I said: If you turn from your sinful ways, then you'll start to experience the manifestation of the LORD's blessings!"

Everyone got on their feet and began clapping, shouting, and applauding the man of GOD.

"Can I get a witness in here this morning? Y'all ain't hear me. I wish I can get someone to say AMEN!"

"Amen, Bishop! Go ahead and preach!"

"Saints, you know me. Y'all know I ain't gonna sugarcoat nothing to you. I'ma give it to you like this here: The Bible said no one can serve two masters. Either you gon love one and hate the other or you gon be devoted to one and despise the other. But you cannot— I'm gonna say it again—you cannot serve both the LORD and be a devil-worshipper at the same time."

When he finished saying that last part, all hell broke loose. People took off their shoes and began running up and down the aisle like they were on fire for Jesus.

"Why y'all looking at me crazy like I said something wrong? I didn't say it; I'm just the messenger. So, don't be mad at me! You have to talk to GOD about that one!"

"Go ahead, Bishop! You ain't saying nothing but the truth!" someone yelled.

"Amen to that!" someone else screamed.

Now, don't get me wrong: Daddy is a beast behind the pulpit. When it's time for him to deliver the message, he lacks nothing in that area. But when it's time for him to apply those same words to his life and be a doer, well…that's when I have a problem. That's where he should be more focused and start practicing the things that he is preaching.

I have never read the Bible, but from what I've heard, it also says, "Do not judge or you, too, will be judged. For in the same way that you judge others, you will be judged and with the same measure you use, it will be measured to you."

So, when my father, Bishop Curtis Jones, starts putting those words that he quotes from the Bible that are acceptable and pleasing to the LORD into action, then that's when I'll start paying attention to his sermons.

Chapter 3: Kelis
Busted and Bribed

When the service was finally over, Raven and I raced to the cafeteria. We looked forward to the trips there every Sunday afternoon. With our tiny hands stuffed with our favorite snacks, we then searched for a seat at our designated table. On this day, we were abruptly interrupted.

"Hey, grandpa," I said between bites.

"Lil' girl, I see you still ain't learned no manners. What I told you about talking with food in your mouth?" Focusing his attention on Raven, he said, "How's grandpa baby feeling?" I don't know if he was trying to be funny or not, but Raven ignored his question and continued taking small bites of the honeybun she was eating. "Baby, let me know what grandpa can get you for Christmas."

"Grandpa, I know what I want for Christmas!" I screamed, answering his question for Raven while she gave me that stare. If looks could kill, I'd be dead right now.

"Chile, I'm not talking to you."

At times, I wondered why our grandpa showed favoritism in loving my sister while hating me. He often gave her special gifts and even went the extra mile on Christmas and birthdays.

"Hypocrite," Raven mumbled.

I was in tune to my own thoughts, but that didn't prevent me from hearing what she called our grandpa.

When he finally realized he was having a conversation all by himself, he left—but not before leaving a pile of candy on the table.

We were born of the same parents, so how could he love one child so much and despise the other? Is this what Jesus meant when He said to love your neighbors as much as you love yourself? We both looked like our mother, except I was the one who was blessed and favored by her light complexion. Raven, on the other hand, was a darker version. Light-skinned girls are what's "in" right now, so in my mind, I look a whole lot better and am prettier than her. Raven and I remind me of the story of Jacob and Esau in the Book of Genesis. The only difference is that she ain't got no birthright to get.

It didn't take long for those feelings of anger, hatred, jealousy, and rejection to get aroused. Putting my thoughts to the side, I told Raven I'd be back. When I entered the sanctuary, no one was in sight. My senses led me to the First Lady's office. I was in total disbelief when I caught her red-handed. My first instinct never fails me. It's one thing to hear shocking news from someone else, but seeing that person bent over counting money from the church's safe is another. I might be young, but there's nothing dumb about me. I stood silently in the doorway and watched as momma counted out some twenties and then tucked them into her bra. She then counted out another set of twenties and a ten-dollar bill and placed that stack into her shoe.

"Mm-Mm," I grunted, interrupting her actions. She turned and stared at me with shame, embarrassment, and guilt written all over her face. Finally coming to her senses, she motioned for me to enter the office.

"Umm, Baby? What have I told you about knocking and waiting for an invitation?"

I know this woman didn't just check me after she was caught stealing money from GOD! I kept my eyes glued to her chest. "What?" she asked, following my gaze. "Oh, that? Haha! Oh, Baby; that's nothing. That's just some change I took out to give to your father."

Now she's really trying my intelligence, I thought—as I glimpsed under her desk at the safe that sat wide open. *Handling the funds is not the First Lady's responsibility, so what was it doing here in her office? And why was she stooping as low as to steal what belongs to the LORD? Momma has a whole lot of explaining to do if she's expecting me to keep quiet about this one!*

"Here, Baby. Just take this and buy something nice for you and your sister. But I want you to promise me something: Promise that you will keep what you just saw between the both of us. You can't say anything to no one, not even your sister. Can you promise me that?"

I shook my head from side to side. I was not only amused; I was totally disgusted that my mother was trying to bribe me to condone her sins.

Chapter 4: Shanece
Molestation Made Me...

No one understands. Not even my own damn husband will ever comprehend my struggles. Before we got married, he knew what he was up against. Hell, he was one of my most loyal clients! Damn. I must admit: The type of money he was spending on me? I wasn't going to tell him no! Then, out of nowhere, this nigga wanna pop up talking 'bout he's saved. Better yet, he got baptized and was ready to marry me! What did he think? I was gon turn down the access to free money? During the years that we were messing around, I always knew I had him. My kitty glittered like gold, and I had him right where I wanted him to be.

Being the First Lady came with a lot of benefits, so when he brought up the topic about becoming a pastor, I said "HELL, YES!" quick, fast, and in a hurry! I was ready to walk down the aisle and have the preacher change my last name! I wear my title to the fullest and dare any of those churchgoers to get in my way. I was given a set of keys to the safe that belongs to The First Baptist Church of Christ and, to add icing to the cake, I was granted full access to Pastor Curtis Jones' bank accounts the day we left the courthouse. Well, I had access to his bank accounts until about a year ago when I showed up to withdraw $5,000.00 from one of his checking accounts, and the teller held onto my driver's license a little too long. Next thing I knew, the officer placed me in the back of a police car. I was charged with all types of fraud—from grand theft to the fraudulent use of a credit card. It took providing proof of my marriage and a whole lot of convincing the judge and state attorney that I was a changed woman before the charges were finally dismissed. A year later, here I am. I have no other options but to be stealing money from the house of God. From what I understand, God is forgiving and doesn't hold grudges against His people, so hell—He'll understand.

My addictions started when I was around 17 years old. I grew up with no father and witnessed the traffic that continuously came and went all hours of the night. It ain't like I ain't know right from wrong. I grew up in the church. Every Sunday morning, bright and early, momma would be up cooking my favorite breakfast and then off to Sunday school we would go. During the week, we would attend Bible study. That was the norm from the time I was a toddler until I turned thirteen. Unlike many of my friends' parents, momma had a great job. Back then, she worked at the hospital as a Registered Nurse. I was the only child, so I was always dressed in the best of the best. I had all the boys in school fighting over me—and all the grown men drooling at the mouth every time they saw me. Whatever I wanted, I got. Momma always made sure of that, but she also made sure always to remind me about my prized trophy.

"No money, no honey," was what she drilled into my brain.

All the luxury spending my mother did abruptly stopped soon after my 13th birthday. Momma got fired from her job, and she was too prideful to ask for help, settle for less, or accept any handouts from anyone. Whatever savings she had was long gone within the first six months.

One day, momma decided she wanted to start her own business. I remember overhearing her say, "Why not use what God blessed me with to get what I want?" That was one of the most popular sayings she would often use around the house. So, starting a business was exactly what she did! Her clientele consisted of judges, lawyers, and doctors. Even the CEO of the hospital where she once worked would show up at our house every weekend to attend a party she called "Lonely Husbands."

In no time, the party grew larger and larger and was a hot topic. Lonely husbands from all over were contacting momma, making their reservations for the upcoming weekends and reserving their spots for ongoing mutual satisfaction. The parties went great for about a year…until one of the wives started following her husband and doing her own investigation. She even got other wives in cahoots with what she was doing. Wives started showing up at our house asking momma to leave their husbands alone, but the money got the best of her. She never took heed of the threats made against her.

One thing led to the next, and the Feds were at our front door. After they ransacked our house, momma was indicted on charges stemming from threats and extortion to numerous counts of fraud. She was eventually sentenced to 18 months in the federal prison system. I was forced out of our house and thrown into the foster care system. Every foster family rejected me for about eight months. Then, momma's brother, my Uncle Dean (the only family member I knew of) came forward and opened up his home to me. He played it nice and safe all the way up until the judge granted him full custody. Back then, Uncle Dean was known as "That Nigga." He was well-respected and highly-spoken of—a young nigga who been in the drug game since the 4th grade and had dropped out of school at the age of thirteen. By adopting me, he felt as if that would have been a sweet cover for his operation and him 'giving back to the community.'

The day after we left the courthouse, he said, "It's time to celebrate!" We went out to eat, and since I only had a few pieces of clothes, he took me shopping and allowed me to pick out whatever I wanted. I loved Uncle Dean more and more each day, but that feeling went out the door almost as fast as it came.

One night, I woke up to find him by my bed with one of his hands between my legs. I opened my mouth to scream but fell silent at the sight of seeing the gun that sat on his lap as his lips covered my mouth.

"Shhh. I won't hurt you. I promise," he whispered. That night, my uncle performed oral sex on me and forced me to return the favor.

Uncle Dean picked up the slack where momma stopped. He kept me laced in all the flyest designers. One day, I came home from school and entered my bedroom. There, I found scented candles burning that lit up the room, along with a light pink piece of lingerie spread across my bed. Minutes later, he stood in my doorway with a broad smile across his face. "Wassup, Baby Girl? Tonight is gonna be special, so take your time getting ready for daddy!"

After he left, I approached the window. The thought of jumping out and running away fled my mind after I witnessed the dogs below that were glued outside my bedroom window. "Lord, please help and carry me through whatever it is that's about to take place," I said out loud.

Minutes later, he entered my room and found me looking out the window. As he got closer to where I stood, the hairs on the back of my neck rose, and nervousness settled in at the thought of the unknown.

"You wanna jump? Go ahead, 'cause they love raw meat," he said while pointing at the three aggressive pit bulls that were chained near my bedroom window. I felt his eyes as they pierced my entire body. He realized then that I wasn't dressed as he'd instructed me to be. "Why ain't you dressed?" he barked, causing me to jump.

I raced over to the bed and gathered up the lingerie that was still laying in the same spot. When I attempted to enter the bathroom, he yelled, "No! Not in the bathroom! You can dress right here!"

Feeling ashamed and hopeless, I slowly began undressing while blocking out all thoughts of his very existence. As soon as I was done getting dressed, Uncle Dean threw me on the bed, ripped off the lingerie, aggressively spread my legs with his rough hands, and took complete control of my body. As he moved closer to my breasts, the smell of cigarettes invaded my nostrils. I remained still with my eyes fixed on one of the first things he ever bought me; a princess clock that hung from the wall. I counted as the seconds ticked by. My body was numb to the pain as he roughly entered me. I blocked out the rape with memories of all the good times I'd once had with momma.

That night, my uncle raped me for what seemed like the longest two hours of my life. After he was finished, this nigga dared to kiss me and wish me a happy birthday! He graduated from molesting to raping me and claiming my body as his prized trophy. I was even introduced to his boys as "his side-piece." Sometimes, he would host house parties and had no problem whatsoever with allowing his boys to take turns raping me.

For the next two years of my life, the abuse continued up until one day, as I was on my home from school and reached the corner of my street, I abruptly stopped once I realized what was taking place right before my eyes. They say that whatever is done in the dark must reveal itself in the light! At that moment, I truly believed that saying.

I witnessed my uncle and his homies being dragged and thrown into the back of police cars that surrounded his house. Reality finally dawned on me that I had nowhere else to go. I wasn't about to get caught up in the system again. With no plans for survival and only the clothes on my back, I made an about-face and headed back in the direction from which I had come. After a week of wearing the same clothes and bouncing around from home to home, sleeping on people's porches, I came up with a plan and made up my mind to execute it. I told myself that hustling is in my blood, so I put on my 'big girl panties' and cleaned myself up.

That was the end of my struggles…or so I thought. God promised that I would have life and have it more abundantly, but He never promised that it would be easy.

I started boosting, and it didn't take long for me to make a name for myself. In no time, I managed to upgrade from being a petty hustler to doing it big. At 17 years old, I was doing well for myself. I managed to finesse a salesman at a local used car dealership into selling me a car AND to put my apartment in his name. Still, no matter what I did or how hard I tried, the demons from my past kept haunting me. With nothing else to lose, I turned to the only thing I knew would help me to escape the pain.

Heading home from the mall after a long day in my newfound profession, I was zoned out at the light when the car behind me honked, interrupting my thoughts of momma. I was too frozen to move. The driver of the other car drove around and stopped on my driver's side. He got out of his car and asked, "Wassup, gorgeous? You good?" Dude stood there witnessing the tears that were streaming down my face. He then opened my door, reached across me, placed the car in park, lifted me, and scooted me over into the passenger's seat. Leaving his car at the light, he climbed behind the wheel of my car and drove into the gas station parking lot that was on the corner.

We sat and talked for about 30 minutes. I learned his name was Choppa, we exchanged numbers, and went our separate ways. Soon after, Choppa and I started dating, and he introduced me to my best friend; a drug called 'C-Class.'

Word on the street was that after my momma left prison, she had checked herself into a halfway house. Not long after that, she started tricking with some nigga named Splash from Pompano who had her working for him. She got infected with the virus, lost hope, and turned to drugs. Splash was her supplier, and he didn't mind because out of all his girls, she was an asset to his business. The money came to a halt when momma had sex with the wrong man, and he became infected with the death ticket. He killed momma and then turned the gun on himself.

After hearing about momma's death, I couldn't take it anymore. I couldn't go on. I no longer wanted to live a life full of anger. I felt my whole world falling apart. While I spent time surveying my life, visions of momma flooded my mind. I wondered in what direction my life was heading or if I would end up like her. I was left in a world full of hatred, bitterness, and cold-hearted individuals. It was me against the world. I turned to what I knew best and vowed to use what my momma had taught me.

When I met Bishop Curtis Jones, he was twenty-five. I was 20 and still in my prime. Not long after we got married, I found out I was pregnant; pregnant with no education, no job, and no pot to piss in or a window to toss it out of. I tried everything to get rid of my pregnancy. When the doctor at the abortion clinic told me I was having twins and that I had waited one month too long, I damn near choked the life outta him. I did the only thing I knew: continued getting high, day in and day out. To my disappointment, I failed to miscarry. My babies were birthed with no defects.

When God has ordained something, His will must be done. No one can get in the way of blocking what God has destined to happen.

Now, here I am at the age of thirty. I'm a married junkie who steals from the Lord and pretends to be the person others want me to be.

Chapter 5: Raven
Grandpa's Special "Love"

Leaving me to myself was the best thing Kelis could have ever done for me. The ride home from church was awkwardly silent. Everyone seemed to be in their own little world, which was very unusual. My family doesn't discriminate. Even after a powerful Sunday morning sermon, they would always seem to find something to argue about.

After getting home and settled in my bed, my mind suddenly drifted back to the reason why, at seven years old, I'm still using the bathroom in my bed. I was five years old when momma got sick and was admitted to the hospital. With daddy at her beck and call, we were forced to stay with our grandpa for two horrible weeks. Whenever grandpa was around, he would always have this creepy expression on his face that made me feel uncomfortable, but who was I to mention it to my parents? They would swear I was lying and tryna be grown. My sister was always too busy begging for something to recognize his flirtatiousness.

The night that grandpa snuck into my room uninvited in the middle of the night, my senses told me that he meant trouble. I smelled his presence even before he made his way to my bed. As he stood there, he tickled my feet, checking to see if I was awake. The smell of alcohol penetrated my room, and from the sound of his slurred speech, I already knew he was drunk.

"Baby, you sleep?" he asked. Too frightened to say a word, I laid still, hoping he would take that as a reason to excuse himself. My silence only made him desire me even more. He moved closer, sat on the edge of the bed, and began to gently massage my back. His hand managed to make its way under the sheet where he cupped one of my butt cheeks in the palm of his hand. I tensed up at his touch. Releasing a sigh, he flinched then said, "Sorry for waking you, Baby Girl. I didn't think you were awake." Ignoring his comment, I threw the covers off me and attempted to get out the bed. He immediately stood, walked to the door, and blocked my exit.

"Baby Girl, I don't wanna hurt you. This can go two ways, and it's up to you. Do it my way, and I'll make sure it goes as smooth as possible. So, come on. Let's play a little game. You must remember you can't be loud 'cause your sister is sleeping in the room next to you. Okay, Baby Girl? It's simple. Do as I say, and everything else will be alright."

I stared at him coldly when he told me to get undressed and get back in the bed. I did as I was told. Grandpa followed suit. Laying across my bed, he did the unexpected when he took my hand, placed it on his manhood, and instructed me to stroke him slowly. As I laid in the bed beside him, I began to question God's existence. Where was He when I needed Him the most? Yes, I believe in Jesus, the Alpha and Omega. Yes, I believe He died on the cross for my sins and rose again on the third day. And yes, I know that He has the power to give and take away. Why didn't God strike grandpa the night he tried to penetrate me? He even had the nerve to dare me to tell anyone, threatening that if I did, there would be consequences and repercussions I would have to pay—and he would make sure of that!

As those words escaped his mouth, I knew what that statement meant. It wasn't to be taken lightly.

I felt torn between love and hate. I wanted to hate God for allowing certain things to take place in my life, but I also loved Him because, like the story of Job, He didn't allow the devil to kill me. I dealt with my attacker and the pain he caused me each time my sister and I visited his house. I would lay down in the exact spot, sweating and crying hysterically. I decided enough was enough and wanted to have a word with God.

"Heavenly Father, I really need you right now. I need some answers from you. I'm at a loss for words and don't know what to say to you. I want you to know that I hate myself, I hate life, but most of all, I despise my grandpa. God, am I wrong for wanting him dead? Am I wrong for how I feel? I don't understand why You allow bad things to happen in my life, but You say You love me. What kind of love is that? I just wanna know why, God? Why me? Why is this happening to me?" Those words were whispered in between sobs as I rocked myself back and forth, trying to ease the pain and find the answers I desperately sought. "Father, I thought You cared for me. So, why my life had to be this way? Jesus, will you please just answer me?"

As I ended my prayer, a sense of relief washed over me. I then heard a voice loud and clear in my room that said, "My child, walk by faith and not by sight. Continue to trust in Me. I will bring you through all the storms in this life. I will never leave you, nor will I ever forsake you. You were called by name because you are My child."

Feeling a bit scared, I turned over on my back and stared at the ceiling. That's when I saw it—my angel, looking down on me. I was too frightened to utter a word. I closed my eyes, and when I opened them again, she was gone. At that moment, I knew for sure that the Great "I Am" was with me.

Chapter 6: Raven
A Right-Now Word

The week went by remarkably fast. To my surprise, there were no bad vibes or interruptions in our house. I was overjoyed about tonight's Bible study 'cause daddy would be preaching, and if anyone knows my daddy like I do, then they know that all hell gon break loose because he doesn't play! He gets down to business whenever he's sharing the Word of God. Tonight was no different. I sat in the front row of the church as I listened precisely to every word the man of God was saying.

"Good evening, Saints. As I sat in my office last night doing some studying and meditating on what I wanted to share with you tonight, I said, 'Lord, what do You want me to tell Your people? Let Your will be done as it will be done in Heaven. You lead, and I will follow behind You.' Right after I finished saying those words, the Lord spoke to me. So, tonight, I'm going to be talking to you about hope. But before I do that, I wanna touch up on a few key points on taking authority when things around you are outta order. You see, it is written in the Word that 'no weapon formed against you shall prosper.' So, people, if the Bible says it, then why don't you believe it, live it, and act on it? Why do we give the enemy the power to trample us? Huh? Can someone agree with me on this one?"

"Amen, Bishop! I agree with you," came the response.

"We have to choose from this day forward to stand on the Word of God. We have to take God at His Word because it is true, alive, and active. It says here in Psalms 35:2 that He is our shield and buckler. Jesus has given us the power and authority to tread on the lion and serpent. We have the sword right here in our hands." He held his Bible high in the air. "This is what we must use to fight our battles. We have the power to defeat the enemy; not to be defeated by him or his little minions. So, let's make up our minds today to look the devil in his face and speak to that sucker in the name of Jesus because, you see, the Lord says that He thrusts out the enemy and says to you, 'Destroy them!' Can I get an Amen?"

Everyone sang in unison, "Yessss, Bishop! Hallelujah, Man of God! Amen!"

"Yes, Bishop! Hallelujah, Man of God! Say that again!" someone screamed from the back.

"You see, God can't work without us. When He left, He gave us our advocate: The Holy Spirit. Once you're a child of the Creator, you're well-equipped with the Holy Spirit. So, don't let no one tell you no foolishness!"

Feeling good, I stood to my feet and yelled for him to keep going. "That's what I'm talking 'bout, daddy!"

"Now, I wanna go a little further as to the real purpose why I was sent to teach this message on hope. There are a lot of people out here today who are losing hope. If I'm speaking to you, then I'm here to tell you that there is hope—a hope that is through the risen King and the blood of Jesus, our Lord and Savior. That hope comes from the One and Only Living God, and there's no other. As sons and daughters of our Heavenly Father, we are victorious. We are more than conquerors. We've been forgiven, and we can choose to walk in a glorious relationship with Christ, our Risen King. We don't have time to sit around complaining or whining about anything. We don't have time to waste and sit around feeling sorry for ourselves. As children of the Most High God, it is time to take back what is rightfully ours."

He paused to let that sink into congregation for a moment before continuing.

"Now, I didn't say we must give up. When Jesus was tempted by Satan, did He quit and allow the devil to defeat Him? Did Jesus quit while He carried the cross? No! So, who are we to quit? God made no failures or regrets. After He created each of us, He was satisfied with all His masterpieces. Saints, I'm telling you that we must hold fast and stand firm on the Word that has been freely given to us, even when our current circumstances are saying otherwise.

"Saints, look at King David. You remember when King David was anointed as the king, right? Well, he didn't have it any easier than none of us. Through adversity and every trial, he knew that God was still in control. Through failures, hardships, in darkness and the light, and in our victories in faith, the Lord is still the same God yesterday, today, and forever. He's not a man that He should lie. His words will not return to us incomplete. That's one check you can write and guarantee that it won't come back void. Please, saints; don't let the devil fool us. Remember that he comes to kill, steal, and destroy. Don't allow him to put fear in your hearts. God did not give us a spirit of fear. We are created with the Spirit of power, love, and a sound mind. We are not to allow Satan to make us timid and wanna give up. When you feel like there's no place else to hide, your back is against the wall, and you've done all that you can do to stand, pick up the armor of God and use it with full force!

"Ephesians 6:13 says after you've done everything to stand on His words, stand on His promises. Don't forget that He's the Great "I Am"—the One who conquered death. Stand on His unchanging grace. Saints, He did it for Joseph when his own blood sold him. He did it for Job when he lost everything, but one thing he never lost was his faith in God. He did it for His disciples. And He surely came through for Ruth. God does not show favoritism. He did it for them, and He will do it for everyone who believes.

"Thanks for coming out tonight and listening as I shared with you the message. Can everyone please stand to your feet as we come to a close?"

I couldn't stop smiling because the Spirit of God was definitely in the house tonight! I felt His presence, and that message hit home. That message was just for me. I was once blind, but now I can see. God was speaking to me tonight. I'm uncertain at this present time, but one day, I will soon get the revelation of the plans and purposes God intended for my life. For right now, I'll allow Him to chisel and mold me to be His perfect vessel.

Chapter 7: Kelis Christmas Joys

With our eighth birthday and Christmas slowly approaching, everyone was full of the holiday spirit. Daddy and momma were outside putting the Christmas lights around the house. Every year, the mayor held a contest; the family with the best-decorated house usually walked away with cash. This has been our same address as long as I've known myself. Our house usually won first place, but last year, the house on the next block decided to step up their game and stole the spotlight. This year, the first-place prize would be $250.00 and tickets for the movies. When momma got word that money was the prize for this year, she had daddy ordering all different types of fancy decorations. She even went as far as decorating the roof! I thought that was the crazy part.

During my years on this earth, I'd never seen someone so in love with money like my mother. From the looks of it, daddy was exhausted from all the work he'd been doing. He has been ripping and running all day while momma sat back barking orders. As long as she was happy, he didn't mind being told what to do. That's what I loved and admired the most about my father; his loyalty, patience, and compassion. For the ones that he loves, there's no limit to what he'll do. Even with that monkey that seems to be riding momma's back, he has never attempted to disrespect or lay a finger on her.

"Kelis! Keeeellllliiiiissssss!" Momma screamed my name.

"Yes, momma; I'm here."

"Girl, how many times I had to holla your name? Are you deaf or something?"

"I wish she would just get to the point," I mumbled underneath my breath as I rested my hand on my hip. My attitude was apparent. I was aggravated the minute I heard her voice. What made her think it would be any different now that I'm standing before her?

"Yes, momma. Why you doing all that? I didn't hear you earlier, so I'm here now."

"Girl, who the hell you dismissing? You better fix them legs before I come fix them for you! Go in the fridge and bring me the pitcher that got the iced tea in it. And bring two glasses."

Boy, I can't wait for my 18th birthday so I ain't gotta put up with her and all the extra drama! When I move out, I'll never return. Hell no! I'll do whatever I have to do to keep a roof over my head.

Hanging up the decorations was not my favorite part of the holiday. By the time I did as my mother asked and got back, Raven was focused on a picture she had of baby Jesus. Adding the final touches, I placed the angel on the tree in its designated spot. Stepping back, I did a double-take and looked at my work.

"I don't know what you smiling for, like you did something," Raven said.

"Can I enjoy the moment for myself without your distraction?" I shot back at her.

On Christmas morning, I was awakened earlier than usual by the smell of freshly-baked gingerbread cookies. I made my way down the stairs and helped myself to a few, along with a tall glass of cold milk. Upon hearing laughter coming from the direction of the family room, I walked in and watched momma and daddy. They were caught up in their moment, sashaying and smiling at each other while *Sweet Lady* blasted through the surround-sound speakers. I was happy to see that for once, they were getting along and enjoying each other. Still, I had to wonder how long the happiness would last. Not wanting to interrupt their happily-ever-after moment, I headed back to the kitchen where Raven sat, stuffing her face with a glass of ice-cold milk and the four cookies that sat on the napkin in front of her.

"What's all that noise I'm hearing?" she asked.

"That's momma and daddy in there dancing, so make sure you don't go in there disturbing their peace." Her eyes widened as those words escaped my lips.

"Ooooo! I wanna see!" Raven squealed, as she ran towards the direction of the music. I attempted to grab her, but I was too late. Soon, she was standing in the doorway—and I was right behind her.

We watched as our parents behaved as if they were teenagers in love with each other for the first time. Not being able to control ourselves, Raven and I made some giggling sounds, which caused them to look in our direction. Like the prodigal son's father, our parents spread their arms wide open, welcoming us to join them.

"How long y'all been there spying on us?" asked momma.

"Not that long," replied Raven.

"Ooooo, momma; she lying!" I screamed.

Huddled in our parents' arms, we danced, laughed, and shared a lot of old memories about the fun times we had.

Later that morning, momma cooked our favorite breakfast: steak and cheese omelets, French toast, scrambled eggs, and sausages. While daddy was prepping dinner, I was consumed with what a normal family should be like.

Daddy asked, "What seems to be occupying your mind, Baby Girl? You've been smiling all morning!"

"Nothing, daddy. I'm just happy." My response prompted tears to form in the corners of my eyes. "This is the best Christmas we've ever had."

Everyone except daddy started crying. Now and then, I could hear him sniffling, and he would turn his head away each time a tear managed to escape from the corner of his eyes.

Our Christmas/birthday celebration was getting better by the minute, especially when it came time to open our gifts. Daddy had bought Kelis and me brand-new laptops. Momma had gotten us brand-new phones. She said we were of the right age where we should have phones of our own, especially with all the craziness that's been happening. She would rather be safe than sorry. The only catch was that we would have to pay our own bills. That meant we had to start doing more than just cleaning our rooms. Daddy chimed in and said that it was time for us to learn the true meaning of responsibility.

Daddy had bought momma a necklace. In return, she had given him a wallet along with a watch. At the dinner table, each of us said our own prayer and gave thanks to our Creator for another year and for bringing us this far.

Chapter 8: Shanece
One Year Later

For the first time in my life, everything around me seemed to be normal. My husband was in such disbelief by my sudden change, he even agreed to walk this journey with me. The decision to enter recovery called for my attention one day when my husband and kids were out. I sat on the floor in my closet with a bottle of pills in front of me as flashbacks from my past invaded my mind. Not being able to fully accept me for who I am and visions of momma's dead body lying in the casket had controlled my life. Her attacker had disfigured her face beyond recognition. I was unable to restrain myself from violently crying and punching holes in the wall.

"Whyyyy, Father? Why did You have to take her away from me? I'm blaming You for everything. What kinda God are You, huh? First, You turn around and let them send my momma away to prison. Then, You let my uncle strip me of my innocence. Now, momma's dead. Well, what's next? I'm not understanding what You're doing in my life. Lord, all I'm asking is that You please help me get through this pain! I just feel like giving up, God. I really do. I cannot go on no more. I need answers."

I paused for a second and suddenly remembered the pills. The solution to my problems that I asked God to fix sat before me. I attempted to grab the pills, but my fingers were unable to grasp the bottle. My hand froze when I heard a voice say, "I knew you before you were born, for I placed you there in your mother's womb. My daughter, I haven't gone anywhere. Wherever you go, there I will always be because you are Mine. I will never leave you, nor will I forsake you."

I looked around trying to locate the direction the voice was streaming from, but no one was there. I stood and asked, "Who's there?" I tiptoed into my bedroom and peeped up and down the hallway. No one was in sight. Not knowing what else to do, I walked back into the closet. This time, I made sure to close the door tightly. When I sat down in the same spot, something was different. The bottle of pills wasn't where I had left it. I soon realized that Christ was in that space with me. He was back! Well, in actuality, He never left me; it was me who had left Him.

I got down on both knees, poured out my heart to Jesus, confessed my sins to Him, and surrendered. From that day forward, I made up my mind to get saved and follow Him as He leads. I've committed to crucifying myself in the flesh and spending time with my Lord and Savior. I even went as far as to receive counseling. I don't like telling my business to people I care nothing about. It took a lot of hard work and dedication, but after some time, those around me started noticing the changes. I was no longer stealing from the church. My husband was my primary support, and we were doing my 12-Step recovery together.

I've been clean for about ten months and, for the first time in my life, I know what it feels like to be loved unconditionally. So many great things were starting to take place in my life. Doors were being opened, as well as some were being closed. People I used to get high with who I once considered friends became my frenemies. People who I thought would be happy for my change were smiling in my face while putting bull's eye Xs on my back.

God came and spoke to me one day as I was seeking His will and purpose for my life. He was using me in many ways. I started my ministry: a home for young girls who have walked in my shoes and are still trying to find themselves. It's a lifelong journey for me. There have been plenty of days when the devil came whispering sweet lies in my head—times when I felt like washing my hands of my new life, throwing in the towel, and giving in to the devil's scheme. But then, I would always hear that still, small voice that reminded me the battle is not mine; it's the Lord's!

Chapter 9: Kelis
Reckless Talk

Unlike most kids my age, I was never given a chance to experience and enjoy my childhood. My circle consisted of my sister and me. We weren't allowed to have friends or sleepovers at our house. I believe that God exists, but attending church was not my cup of tea. Most people enjoyed it, but me? I despised it. I find it very hard to believe that this 'God' would allow hurt and pain to be inflicted on my life, so why was I the one being chastised and treated like the black sheep of the family?

"Sister, get your Bible. I found something very interesting we could talk about," Raven said, taking a seat on my bed.

"Well, hey to you, too! You're welcome to come in," I replied sarcastically.

"Girl, why you looking at me all crazy like that? Get your Bible and come on."

"Who said I was interested in what the hell you're reading?"

"Girl, what's your problem? I can clearly see that you done woke up on the wrong side of the bed."

"Why I had to wake up on the wrong side of the bed 'cause I don't wanna hear what you got to say? But now that we on that subject, you know what's really wrong with me? I'm so sick and tired of you and daddy forcing me to read the Bible. I don't wanna know nothing about Jesus. I couldn't care less to know about Jesus' crucifixion 'cause to me, all that is just a bunch of fairytale lies. So, please: I'm begging you to keep all that drama to y'all's self."

"Wowww! You been holding that one in for a minute. Let me get away from you so when God does strike, it won't touch me!"

"Why you always tryna be funny?"

"Do you see any smiles on my face? I don't know about you, but I don't play games with God 'cause He…"

"Just shut the hell up and stop it with the madness! Get outta my face!" Raven looked at me with shock written all over her face. Tears began to fall. "Oh no, Raven. I'm sorry. Why are you crying? I'm so sorry. I…I…I don't know…" My voice trailed off as I paused and thought of my next choice of words. "It's not your fault; it's mines. I just hate life. I'm very angry at God. At times, I don't even believe He exists. I hate myself. At times, I really wish momma did abort us…well, abort ME."

"I understand how you feel. It's okay to be angry at God, but…"

"Ain't no 'but.' I hate me. At times, I wish that I was dead or not even here at all."

"Sis, I'm sorry you feel that way, but you can't talk like that. I know that you're mad and all, but no matter how you're feeling, He still loves you. Now, THAT'S unconditional love."

"Jesus loves me? Girl, you must be crazy! Just shut up 'cause right now, you ain't making no sense. Are you serious? I…I don't understand you and daddy about this Jesus mess."

"You're right. You don't understand—and you probably never will."

"We're twin sisters, Raven, but we ain't the same. It's obvious we have different interests. This 'Jesus' y'all keep talking about died for y'all, not for me."

"You talking reckless. What makes you think you're so different from me? He died for you, too. He doesn't show favoritism. He died for the whole world, but it's up to us to make that decision to choose Him. God sent His One and Only Son into the world to save us from death. So, whoever believes in Him will not perish but have everlasting life. You ever heard that saying "People in Hell want ice water"? Well, Kelis, I don't want you to die and go to Hell because you didn't make the right choice. Look. It says right here in John 3:6 that whoever believes in the Son has eternal life, but whoever rejects the Son will not see life, for God's wrath will remain on them."

"I never said that God ain't real, Raven. I mean, I know that He exists. Hell, where is God when bad things happen to people? Where is He when you hear about kids being hurt? I guess He be too busy tending to them damn flocks. He ain't got time for the sheep."

"Honestly, I can't really answer those questions. The only thing I can say is that the God I serve is a mighty God. He's supernatural and has the power to do anything He wants to do.

Romans 8:28 says that in all things, God works for the good of those who love Him, who have been called according to His purposes. He's Omnipresent—meaning He's capable of being everywhere at once. There's no location in this universe that He doesn't inhabit. He's Omnipotent—meaning He has the power over everything. He gives us life and, at the same time, He can take it away. And He's Omniscient—meaning He knows everything before it even happens. Nothing happens by surprise to God.

"Psalms 139:5 says that before a word is on my tongue, the Lord knows it completely. And look at what verse 13 through 16 says: "For You created my inmost being, You knit me together in my mother's womb. I praise You because I am fearfully and wonderfully made; Your works are wonderful, I know that full well. My frame was not hidden from You when I was made in the secret place when I was woven together in the depths of the earth. Your eyes saw my unformed body; all the days ordained for me were written in Your book before one of them came to be.""

I had to stop Raven right there. "I'm glad you know the Bible like you do, but I don't. Although it actually sounds interesting, I still can't understand it. If God knows all this about us, then why in the hell He be allowing bad stuff to happen? I'm sorry, but I'm not getting it. Then again, this 'God stuff' ain't for me 'cause I'm not understanding Him."

"It's not for you or me to understand, Kelis. That's where our faith comes in. He's Almighty and Sovereign. He does whatever is pleasing to Him. For instance, you can have someone who has hurt you, but you prayed to God about the situation. He might turn around and bless that person. So, in the back of your mind, you're like, 'Yeah, I done gave it to God. Now, watch how He gon' strike you for messing with one of His kids.' No, Sis; God doesn't operate like that 'cause that same person might be a child of God as well, and they simply messed up. They can turn around, pray about it, and ask Him for forgiveness. God can then turn around and grant them grace and mercy. We're not perfect. We're gonna make mistakes. Think about it: What if it was you who hurt someone? Would you like for that person you hurt to pray and want God to cause harm to you? I'm sure your answer is no. So, you see, it goes both ways. That goes to show you that whatever He feels like doing, He's gonna do it. I'm saying all of that to get to this point: His ways and thoughts are always higher than ours. You will never figure Him out. The only thing you should do is accept Him, build a relationship with Him, and watch how He moves in your life. No matter how you feel, He still loves you unconditionally and wants to be your Father. The question is: Will you accept Him?"

"I don't know, Raven. I can't answer that right now." Tears began to spill from my eyes. "I need some time to think about it."

"Okay, Sis. I'm not forcing you. That's a decision you will make when you're ready. I will pray for you that you won't wait until it's too late because tomorrow isn't promised to no one. The Bible says if you hear His Word, do not harden your heart." Raven stood to leave. "I'm going downstairs to see what momma is doing. Let me know if you wanna talk some more. I'll be here for you." Those were her final words before she disappeared from my sight.

I closed the door behind her, laid across my bed, and allowed the conversation to linger in my mind. One part of me wanted to give Jesus a chance, but I'm afraid of what might happen next.

Chapter 10: Raven
The Life-Changing Message

"Good morning. Can everyone please stand to your feet and let's say a word of prayer before we enter into the presence of the Lord? Heavenly Father, we come together before You in the name of Your precious Son, Jesus Christ. Father, we are choosing to confess our sins to You—sins of omission and sins of commission, whether known or unknown by words, deeds, or thoughts. We ask You to forgive and cleanse us from all unrighteousness. We enter Your gates with thanksgiving and Your courts with praise. This is the day that You, Lord, have made. We will rejoice and be glad in it. Holy Spirit, we welcome You in this house today. Lord, we ask You to pour out Your anointing and cause Your anointing to break the yokes and bondages of principalities and rulers in dark places. Lord, we ask You to bless this service today. We love You, Lord. We worship You. We magnify Your Holy name. We give You thanks. We praise and glorify Your blessed name in Jesus' name. Everyone say 'Amen.'"

"Amen," the congregation shouted.

"Now, if you can look to your neighbors, saints—not your next-door neighbor, but the ones standing next to you—God said to love your neighbor as you love yourself. He never said to only love the person who lives next door to you. In this case, He's speaking of everyone. So, can you look at that person next to you and welcome them? Amen?"

"Amen," everyone sang in unison. The congregation began greeting one another with hugs and kind words. The scene was surreal.

"Alright, now. Y'all can go ahead and have a seat. Saints, I won't keep you for long. I promise. Trust me: I know y'all wanna go home and eat some of that oxtail, fried chicken, and rice you done made."

"Amen to that!" someone from the back of the church said. The congregation chuckled and agreed with daddy's corny joke.

"I would like for you to go with me to the Book of Daniel 3:18. We are now living in a time when people's favorite word is "Why?" When things start to go bad or are unexpected, we love to ask God why. "Why, God? Why this? Why that?" Our favorite one is, "Why me?" But you see, saints; the question is what are you going to do when you have prayed, and He doesn't answer your prayer exactly how you're expecting it to happen? Are you going to give in and give up or are you gonna be mad at God? I know what I'm going to do! So, I would like to know what you are going to do? That's the question I would like to ask today.

"You see, in the Book of Daniel, those three brothers—Shadrach, Meshach, and Abednego—were told by King Nebuchadnezzar that if they do not bow down and worship his golden god images, they would be immediately thrown into the blazing furnace. Scripture goes on to say that those brothers refused to bow down and worship an idol. They didn't run to God and ask, 'Why us? Why did You put us in this situation?' Instead, what they said to the king was, 'We do not need to defend ourselves before you in this matter. If we are thrown into the blazing furnace, the God that we serve can deliver us from your Majesty's hand.' You see it in the Scriptures for yourself, saints. No matter what the outcome would be, they kept their eyes on the Lord. Never once did they take their eyes off Him. Never once did they question God or ask 'Why me?'

"Let me tell you something: The minute we give the devil room and allow him to whisper little, crazy thoughts in our ears, that's when he's going to step in and attack. In the midst of going through the fire, Job kept his faith. In the midst of going through the fire, Joseph stood firm in what he believed. And in the midst of going through the fire, those three brothers didn't lose hope because they already knew that the God they served is bigger than the god King Nebuchadnezzar presented. But guess what? The Lord didn't stop the king from doing what he planned to do. God allowed them to be thrown into the blazing furnace. Now, let me tell you something: God does what He wanna do! Yes, He could have saved them right away from the hands of the king, but He said, 'No. Go ahead, King Nebuchadnezzar. Do what you do because I have a better plan. I'm going to show you today who's in charge.' That type of faith doesn't come easy. It takes a lot of praying and studying your Word day in and day out to develop that type of faith and have a relationship with Jesus—a faith like that of those three brothers comes by eating daily of the Word, meditating, and fasting.

"Ohhh, but saints: It didn't stop there! If you would go to verse 19, it says, 'Even if He does not, we want you to know, your Majesty, that we will not serve your gods or worship the image of gold you have set up.' Now, that's what you call being bold for the Lord! They were very courageous men of God! Now, let's take a look at verse 25 and see what it says. 'Look! I see four men walking around in the fire, unbound and unharmed.' Ain't that something? Open up your mind with me and imagine a blazing furnace, as hot as it can be. Now, just picture you standing there bearing witness as the three men were thrown into the fire. You're expecting them to be burned alive and later found dead, right? Then, all of a sudden, another eyewitness steps forward to see what's going on. He yells that he sees four men walking around in the fire like nothing ever happened. Let me inform you of this: The fourth man they saw was an angel of the Lord. What I'm tryna say is even though the Lord hadn't answered their prayers as they were expecting or how they thought He would, they stood secure and firm on the Lord and His words. Throughout the end of the chapter, they came out of that fire without a single hair on their heads singed or their robes smelling like smoke. Their bodies were untouched by the flames. King Nebuchadnezzar gave praise to the Living God because he saw with his own eyes that the Lord was their Deliverer. The king and his advisers were amazed to know that he did, indeed, order that the furnace be heated seven times hotter than usual. To know that those three brothers were firmly tied but yet went through the fire and were not burned is truly miraculous!

"Saints, I'm here to tell you not to give up. When you've prayed and haven't yet gotten your answer, don't give up on God. Don't give up on yourselves. Keep fighting. Continue pushing. Fight like it doesn't make sense. You gotta stand still under pressure. You have to hold fast and persevere. After you've done all of that, stand firm on the Word of God, and He will see you through. He will fight for you just like He did for those three brothers. There's nothing that's impossible or too hard for the Lord. With Him, all things are possible. Do not give up. I'm warning you right now: Do not quit. You are on the winning side. Let's all stand, shout, and make some noise in the house of the Lord! Your breakthrough is right around the corner! Your blessings are on the way! I SAID TO MAKE SOME NOISE IN THIS PLACE!" Daddy barked into the mic as the congregation loudly rejoiced. Some people began to cry tears of joy.

"Can somebody give Jesus a shout-out? Come. Come to the altar," daddy said while motioning for the lady standing across from me to approach him. "No one understands what you're going through. Let me pray for you. Let me remind you that your God is bigger than what you're going through right now. Call on His name. Say 'Jesus!' Say it! Say it again! Jesus! Jesus! Jesus! Yes, keep saying His name over and over. There's power in that name all alone. Let it fall like rain, Jesus! Ohhh, yesss! Hallelujah, Jesus! Call on Him! Tell Him how much you need Him. Hallelujah! Hallelujah! Praise the Lord, everybody! Woman of God; open your eyes. The Lord said you need to call Him by His name. Don't be afraid. Open up your mouth and scream His name! Look at me. Look! Look at me! He's able! He loves you! Whatever it is, trust Him at His word. He can fix it. You can't handle it. You can't carry it. God said to let it go! In the name of Jesus: Free your mind. Trust Him. He wants you to stop giving it to Him and then taking it back. You can't keep going back and forth like that. Give it to Him and leave it there. Today is the day of redemption. Holy Ghost, let Your fire fall on this woman right now! Say 'Jesus'! Call His name! I want you to continue saying His name!"

The woman began praising the Lord in earnest. She was soon caught up in the Spirit.

"Every hurt, every pain, every struggle—release it right now, in the name of Jesus. It is done. It's over. You have been set free. Do you believe? Look at me. Do you believe that all your problems are gone? The Lord wants you. Young lady, you have a special calling on your life, and God is patiently waiting for you to surrender to Him. Break down the barriers. Break down the pain, the abuse, and the rejections. In the blood of the resurrected King, in the mighty name of Jesus, God says you've been set free! I plead the blood of Jesus Christ over your life, from the crown of your head to the soles of your feet, over your finances, over your health, over your family, and over and inside your home. Come on, children of God. Close your eyes and let's pray. Father, who art in Heaven, I pray that if there's someone in the house today who hasn't accepted You to be their Lord and Savior, that You will soften their heart and that they will leave here today saying "YES!" to Your Son. We thank You for this message and pray that You will see us through the rest of this week as we keep our eyes fixed on You—the Author and Perfecter of our faith. And all God's people say 'Amen.' Thank you for coming out and joining me. Thank you, Jesus."

My decision was completely made to be genuinely devoted to the Lord. I refuse to allow my current hurt and pain to determine my future. I will no longer allow grandpa to interfere with my blessings or determine who God has created me to be.

Chapter 11: Raven
It Cost Me My Virginity

"How's my two most precious daughters doing this morning? What? Why y'all staring at me like I said something wrong?"

"Mommy, why you being so nice? Are you dying or something?"

"Chile, hush. Ain't nobody in this house dying—at least not anytime soon. Y'all looking at me crazy like I can't be nice!"

"No, it's not that you can't be nice; we just ain't used to the new you."

"Well, I ain't gon even lie: I didn't do it on my own. I have to give God all the glory for the work He's doing in my life."

"God?" Kelis asked in disbelief, shocked by our mother's statement.

"You heard me loud and clear and, if you didn't, open up your ears. Yes, I said 'GOD.' He's been working on me, and I must admit:

It sure feels good! Now, any more interruptions before I say what I originally wanted to say?"

"If you say so," Kelis mumbled. By the look of our mother's facial expression, she wanted so badly to respond. I was surprised at her next move.

"Me and y'all's father will be leaving tonight."

"What?" Kelis squealed. "Who's gonna babysit us?"

"I'll get to that part when you let me finish saying what I have to say. As I was saying…" She shot a quick look at Kelis before going on. "We're leaving for our anniversary, so y'all gotta go to grandpa's house for a month until we get back."

"Mommy, you can't be serious. I don't know about Raven, but I don't wanna go to his house—especially not for a whole month!"

"You better watch that tone of voice," daddy said.

Ignoring his comments, Kelis rolled her eyes at our father. "Mommy, why can't we stay here in the house by ourselves? It ain't like you haven't done it before."

"That's different. Besides, we gonna be gone for a whole month. Ain't nobody got time for CPS being all up in my business. I'm not taking any chances with y'all staying home alone. Finish eating your food and go pack your bags. Make sure you pack everything you're gonna need 'cause I ain't giving Nate my house keys." Our mother barked her final orders as Kelis stormed up the stairs, making sure to slam her bedroom door. That caused me to flinch. I remained seated and stared blankly at the remaining food that sat on the plate before me. "Why you still sitting here? You, too! Go upstairs and get your things together so I can drop y'all off."

Later that night at grandpa's house, I sat outside on the balcony and prayed silently to God, asking for protection as He allows the month to go by as quickly and smoothly as possible.

As soon as I ended my prayer, the familiar smell of alcohol flooded my senses. My body immediately got cold as he moved in closer and stood to the left of where I sat. "Hey! There you go! I've been looking all over the house for you. Why don't you come on inside? Besides, it's too late to be sitting out here like this," grandpa said.

"I'm just out here spending some time with God."

"There's no particular place you have to be to talk to God. You can talk to Him in your room. Come on, Baby Girl. Let's go. I don't want you out here like this by yourself," he said as he stood and held the door open, waiting for me to enter.

During the weeks to come, grandpa never approached me sideways. We barely exchanged words with each other, except for the times he took us to the beach and movies. At times, Kelis seemed distracted by whatever thoughts seemed to be occupying her mind. At one point, I noticed that grandpa was ignoring her as if she didn't exist while paying special attention to me. It was a strange feeling witnessing his reactions when she would ask him to buy her something.

What happened to be a great summer turned out to be a great disaster a week after our parent's return. After taking a long, hot shower, I opened the door to my bedroom and found grandpa sitting on my bed naked with a half-bottle of gin in his left hand.

"UGH!" I gasped, damn near choking on my own breath. "What do you want?"

"Close the door."

"No. Not until you first tell me why you're in here."

"Oh no; you do NOT wanna do this. Not now. What you think? You were gonna come over to my house and freely spend my money? 'No money; no honey.' Ain't that y'all's favorite line? Well, guess what? I spent my money, so now I'm gonna need some honey. Close the door and do what I tell you to do—and remember what I told you."

"Yeah, yeah: If I tell anyone, they won't believe me, and you would kill my sister. And why is it so quiet in here? Where is she?"

"Don't worry about her. She's perfectly fine in the other room, looking like Sleeping Beauty. With my special medicine, she won't be able to hear a thing."

"What? You're sick! What did you do to my sister?!"

A creepy smile crept across his face as the words exited his lips. "Yeah, you know; some of my special remedy for times like this. Come here to your granddaddy and give me some suga. I'm not gonna do anything to you. I promise."

I stood still in the doorway and gazed down the hallway. My eyes rested on my sister's room. I saw that her door was closed tightly. Interrupting my thoughts, he yelled, "I SAID TO COME HERE...NOW!" Not wanting to upset him any longer, I closed my door and slowly walked over to him. He began staring at my breasts for a moment before he allowed his hands to freely roam up and down my arms. Finally, he rested them on my hips. Grabbing my left hand, he pulled me in closer to where he sat, causing the towel to freely hit the floor. He then picked me up and tossed me onto the bed, causing my head to bang against the headboard. He got on top of me, wrapped his hand around my neck, and began choking the life outta me. With his free hand, he forced my legs apart. On that night—five months before my 10th birthday—I was zoned out, staring at the ceiling…as my grandpa stole from me my virginity.

I laid on my back with a pillow covering my face, holding back the tears that so badly wanted to escape as I listened to his huffing, puffing, and grunting. When he was done, he laid still right on top of me. At that moment, I recalled a sermon when daddy preached, "What Will You Do When God Doesn't Answer Our Prayers Exactly as We Would Want Him To?"

He answers them accordingly—when He's ready.

Chapter 12: Raven
The Misery Must End

Several weeks later, I found myself feeling worthless and ashamed to face anyone—especially myself. I was confined (by choice) to my bedroom. Most nights, I would cry myself to sleep and ask God, "Why?" Why did I have to endure this? Why did You spare my life? Why did my life have to be the way it is? And why did I have to be born to the parents I now have?" I wanted revenge. I badly wanted to pay back my grandpa for what he had done to me. I felt trapped inside of my body and felt there was no one I trusted to talk to about what happened. I was carrying a heavy burden all alone.

Different ideas kept playing in my head. Immediately, I started to think of ways to execute my plan. I wanted him dead, so maybe I would wait until he's asleep and set his house on fire. Then again, perhaps I would serve him a dose of his own medicine and feed him the same poison he gave my sister, but give it to him in excess. Better yet, I recalled seeing the code to daddy's safe where he kept his gun. I know for sure THAT would put an end to this misery. The voices in my head kept telling me to pray, but at that moment, I didn't want God to be all up in my business. Tears began spilling down my face as I got down on my knees. During my prayer, I received an answer from the Lord.

"For I know the plans I have for you, declares the Lord, plans to prosper you and not to harm you; plans to give you hope and a future."

I remember reading that scripture, but never really paid much attention to the depths of the words until the moment God spoke them to me. He made me a promise! Whatever those words meant…whatever those plans are, I would sure love to know if this chapter of my life was ordained in His Book and, if so, I badly needed to have a face-to-face conversation with the Lord.

It hadn't dawned on me that I hadn't eaten anything until my sleep was interrupted by the aroma of momma's famous Sunday morning breakfast. I exited my room and slowly approached the stairs, descending one at a time. The closer I got to the kitchen, the more I felt the hunger pains sting my stomach. I stood in the doorway to the kitchen and witnessed from afar as momma removed the pancakes from the oven and placed them on each designated plate. I counted four plates on table mats. A smile crept across my face as I thought of how beautiful momma looked in the kitchen and how God must have told her I was beginning to feel my stomach touching my spine. Sensing my presence, she turned to face me. With one hand on her hip and the other with a fork in hand, she blankly stared at me. Her eyes roamed various places of my body.

"What, Mom?"

"Don't 'What, Mom?' me! You can't say good morning? That's what! I ain't sleep with you last night and you coming down here like I told you to stay glued in your room not wanting to eat. Now, here you are—standing there looking like one of them lil Ethiopian kids."

"I'm so sorry, Mommy. You're right. Good morning."

"Mmmhhh. You sure look like you've been starving. You looking like you can eat a whole pig right about now."

"You read my mind correctly. Which plate is mine? I'm so hungry!"

"Hold on. Don't touch nothing on this table."

"Come on, mommy: I'm starving!"

"Yeah, I bet! After you've been stuck in that room for what? Two whole weeks? I knew you'd be coming down here to join us sooner or later."

"Who told you that? God? You claim He always telling you something."

That joke cracked her up. Even I had to laugh at that one 'cause lately, all she'd been talking about is how God told her not to do something and how He told her to give someone a message. It's always "God this" and "God that." God really need to go ahead and tell her the winning numbers for the lottery!

"Mommy, where everyone else at?"

"Oh, they went to put gas in the truck so we ain't gotta worry about stopping on our way to church. You coming down here having a full conversation, but you sure are smelling funky. I hope you already done brushed your teeth and washed your hands so that you can help me finish setting the table."

About 10 minutes after we put the full plates on the table, daddy and Kelis came walking through the door, laughing like they were really enjoying themselves.

When we all sat down at the table, daddy took his position and blessed the food. By the time everyone said 'Amen,' I was already face down in my plate and about to tackle my second pancake. That's when I realized they were all staring at me with their jaws dropped, mouths wide open. "Why y'all staring at me like I did something wrong?" I asked.

"You're sitting there eating like a homeless person on Thanksgiving," Kelis responded.

"Ha, ha, ha. You have jokes, huh?"

Mommy chimed in, "Kelis, hush—and worry 'bout your own plate."

"Well, mommy, can you at least tell her to eat with her mouth closed?"

"Girl, I said to be quiet. You have the nerve to tell someone else how to eat when you be around here eating with stuff dropping from your mouth like I need to get you a personalized bib!"

We all thought momma's joke was funny…except for Kelis.

She tried to make me feel bad, but now the joke's on her. I felt bad for my sister though, 'cause we all knew that mommy was saying nothing but the truth. Still, I knew she was embarrassed. I couldn't control myself, though. I had to laugh at how fast the tables turned.

Chapter 13: Raven
"Yes, Lord!"

During this Sunday's morning service, I decided to sit in the front pew while Kelis sat three rows behind. Across from where I sat was grandpa, sitting with that same devious facial expression like before. My eyes rested on him for about five seconds. He must have felt my stare because that's when he turned and met my gaze. He actually dared to wink his eye at me! I wasn't a bit intimidated by his gesture. I turned my attention to the man of God who was standing at the pulpit delivering a very powerful message.

"Saints, in case you didn't know, there's a big difference between reading and studying the Word. You see, when you just read the Word, you're not doing anything spectacular. Look at it like this: It's the same as if when you do something wrong, and then you're caught red-handed by your father. When he decides to have a talk with you, you're there just to be there because technically, you don't have a choice. Meanwhile, you're not truly listening or paying attention to anything that he's saying. The words are going in one ear and out the other. On the other hand, when you're studying the Word, in the midst of that, you're also meditating. You're eating the Word. You're soaking it all in. You're also learning about your Creator. You're leaning His ways and knowing His likes and dislikes. By doing so, you're starting to enjoy the things you're learning because it gives you joy and you tend to find peace. That's what's called having a personal relationship with your Lord and Savior—not to be confused with infatuation. In that relationship, you're so in love, you know that you can't live without Him. People might think that you're a bit crazy but I want to tell you something, saints: We were made for the Lord, not to please humanity. So what if they think you got some loose screws up there! Keep being on a high for Jesus! Now, I have a question for my married folks. Ha, ha! I already see it now. I can already see on y'all's faces, wondering what's coming next, huh?"

A few people laughed and clapped their hands. "Amen, Bishop!"

"I ain't even going there with y'all today," daddy said jokingly. He quickly returned to his serious mode, picking up where he left off. "How many of y'all in here today can say that when you first met your wife or husband, you went straight to bed with them? Yeah, go ahead! Tell the truth and shame the devil! Come on, now. You ain't gotta be ashamed. Stand up and be grown about it! The whole point I wanna make here is that you don't typically just meet someone, jump in the bed, and then get married the next day. You have to know that person, saints. Y'all have to spend time with each other. Go on dates. Learn about them. Maybe even write a few letters. But once you start vibing with that individual, that's when you start developing feelings. That's the same with Jesus. If you've studied your Bible, you'll see that all throughout the Word, God loves to speak on forgiveness. That word is very important to Him. We're living in a world today where people do not like to forgive one another. They enjoy the feeling of having a grudge and holding onto what the next person has done to them. Next thing you know, that one thing leads to hatred, anger, resentment, and even bitterness. Now, you're walking around with burdensome, heavy loads on your back. Jesus told us that we should forgive our brothers and sisters—not seven times, but seventy-seven times. Keep in mind that Jesus didn't say, 'Oh, you can forgive only those you wanna forgive and up to as many times as you would like.' When He spoke those words, He was speaking of everyone, including me. Now, some of you might be saying, 'Well, Bishop, what if I already done forgave them once but they keep hurting me over and over? What should I do?' Jesus forgave you all those times you kept sinning and hurting Him over and over again, right? He forgave you when He died on the cross for you, right? He forgave your past sins—the ones you've already committed. He's so great that He's already forgiven our future sins, too—even the ones we know nothing about. He's even forgiven all who have crucified Him. So, you tell me: If God can do that for us, then why can't you offer the same gesture of love for our dear brothers and sisters, huh? What makes us so different?

"Yes, I do understand that the pain hurts. I understand that you may get tired of forgiving someone. I know all about those feelings—and so does Jesus. We must remember that we're not doing it for that person; forgiveness is for ourselves, to release us from the heavy load and free us from every stronghold in our lives. When we forgive, we're not giving the devil any foothold in our lives. Throughout the Bible, the word 'forgiveness' is mentioned over 50 times! If anyone is born again of the imperishable seed, each time that we sin, the Holy Spirit convicts us. I'm here to tell you: It is not a great feeling at all. It's one of those feelings when you're made to feel so terrible for what you've done that you have to run to God quick, fast, and in a hurry. By faith, when you pray, you believe that He who is just and faithful will forgive you, right?"

"Praise God!" flowed throughout the sanctuary.

"Well, that is how we are to be with our dear brothers and sisters. The Lord gives us grace and mercy that we don't deserve. We ought to administer to others that same grace and mercy, even if we think they don't deserve it. It's not about what we think. If that was the case, because Adam and Eve sinned in the Garden of Eden, we deserve to die. But God didn't do that. He gave us a new life when He sent His Only Son, Jesus Christ—who was without sin—to be the sacrificial Lamb for us. Our Savior was severely beaten by those who once said they loved Him. They hollered, 'Crucify Him!' They spat in His face. Can you imagine, saints, what Jesus endured for us simply because He loves us so much?

"If you would turn with me to the Book of Isaiah 53:4-6, it says, 'Surely, He took up our pain and bore our suffering, yet we considered Him punished by God, stricken by Him, and afflicted. But He was pierced for our transgressions. He was crushed for our iniquities, the punishment that brought us peace was on Him, and by His wounds, we are healed.' We are like sheep that have gone astray, saints. Each of us has turned to our own way, and the Lord has laid on Him the iniquity of us all. If you've not read that entire chapter, I strongly encourage you to do so. Read and meditate on the words 'Amen,' 'Praise the Lord,' 'Our Most High God,' and 'The Creator of the Universe.' I pray that someone in here today received this message.

"Before I close out, I would like to open the altar to anyone who'd like to come. Is there anyone in the house of the Lord today who felt that message and knows the Lord was speaking directly to you? If you've been running from God and you're ready to surrender, come on down. If you've been saying no all your life, you're not here by mistake. Come to the altar. He's been patiently waiting on this day to come when you would finally make up your mind and say yes to Him. The angels in Heaven are rejoicing right now! If you've had family members who have died and gone to Heaven, they are looking down and smiling right now. This is the time all of them have been waiting for. Don't be ashamed. Jesus doesn't require much. It's very simple: All you have to do is pray this prayer out loud. Romans 10:9-

10 says, 'If you declare with your mouth, Jesus is Lord, and believe in your heart that God raised Him from the dead, you will be saved; for it is with your heart that you believe and are justified, and it is with your mouth that you profess your faith and are saved.' Come on down with me. Amen. Glory to God! Sayyy yesss! Open your mouth and sayyy yesss! Will your heart say yes? There's nothing to be afraid of; the Lord said if you deny Him in front of man, He will deny you in front of His Father. There's nothing spectacular you have to do to earn this gift of salvation. It is freely given to you when you say, 'Yes, Lord! If you lead me, I will obey and follow.' All God wants is a sincere 'yes.' Don't be afraid. Tell the Lord, 'Yes! I wanna do it Your way!' He accepts you for who you are. He's calling you to come to Him with the mess that you are. He can still use you! He can use the broken vessel that you are to do His will and for His glory. Don't worry about who's watching you. Don't worry about who's talking or who's gonna laugh at you. Just say, 'Yes, Lord! Here I am! Take my hand!" John 1:11-13 clearly reads: 'He came to that which was His own, but they did not receive Him; but to those who believed in His name, He gave the right to become children of God—children born not of natural descent, nor of human decision or a husband's will, but born of God.'"

Unaware of the movements in my body, I was led by the Holy Spirit to approach the altar. For the first time, I took the chance of inviting Jesus into my life, not only as Lord of my life but as my personal Lord and Savior.

That was the start of a new beginning.

Chapter 14: Kelis
Deadly Assault Was the Case That They Gave Me

It was my first day back to school, and I was already into some drama with the Jamaicans who called themselves the Chromazz British. The Chromazz crew consisted of three best friends I've been knowing since the 2nd grade. These girls have zero-tolerance for foolishness. They are known for fighting as a trio and carrying razors under their tongues.

I can recall the one time I saw them in action, fighting another girl. They beat her so bad, she had to get reconstructive surgery on her face—and she lost a few teeth. Everyone knew who her attackers were, but was too terrified to say a word. That's why, when the police came around and started questioning everyone, I made sure to stay in my lane.

In my neighborhood, everyone minds their own business, except for a few stick-up kids from around the way. They quickly learned their lesson the hard way after they were dealt with accordingly. The word on the streets was that one stick-up kid used to work for some man named Timeless—the father of the leader of the British crew. Back then, Timeless was the second in command of the biggest drug dealer, until he was sent up the road. Now, he's released after doing a 20-year bid. Even while he was locked up, his boss man, Bullet, was supplying him with all the drugs he needed to get the job done. Timeless had Warden Long exactly where he needed him, which allowed his operation to flow smoothly from behind bars. He didn't waste any time when he started messing around with one of the C.O.s. Feelings got involved, and the C.O. ended up getting pregnant. Timeless convinced her to quit her job, and he's been holding her down ever since. A year before his release, Bullet got sick and was only given six months to live. They said he ended up dying one month before Timeless' release date, but in his will, he turned everything over to Timeless. People were confused and wondered how the hell Timeless was so lucky to inherit the fortune he was given. They later found out that Timeless was Bullet's only child—his only living family member, at that. With Bullet out of the picture, Timeless took over. He fired every existing worker, gathered a team of his own, and took over the operation. Later, he changed the crew's name to The Jamaican Kartels.

"Wassup, Plain Jane?"

"Who the hell you talking to like that?"

"It definitely ain't none of us 'cause we don't come to school looking like how you be dressing."

"What's wrong with my clothes? I don't see nothing wrong with what I'm wearing."

"Uhh…so, you don't see that you look like you be shopping at one of those garage sales?" Some of the other students started to gather around. They know how the British crew gets down, so they came over expecting to see some action. "And you tryna be down with us? Coming up in here like you fresh off one of those banana boats I'm always hearing my daddy talk about," the leader of the crew said.

That last comment caused an uproar. Everyone was laughing and making movements like they were paddling a boat. I hung my head in shame and reached my 6th-period class just in time before the last bell rang. I watched the clock for the entire hour and counted as each minute slowly ticked by. Before class was dismissed, I was already out of the building, getting a head-start before all the other students were dismissed. Two minutes into my journey, a familiar voice screamed, "Plain Jane! Where you think you going?" Recognizing the voice, I ignored her and kept my eyes fixed on the view ahead. "Aye! Slow down! Why you in such a hurry?" she yelled louder.

Knowing what they can do, I started running towards my destination. That made matters worse. I didn't make it far before I felt someone grab me by the hair and yank me backward. We both fell to the ground. I laid flat on my stomach while the three girls stood hovering over me. "Why you run, Ms. Bad and Bougie? Why you run, huh? Don't be scared now. What happened to all that attitude and mouth you had earlier?"

I stayed laying in the dirt and made no sound, hoping they would just leave. The trio then started kicking me in the head, sides of my stomach, and any parts of my body that were visible and in their reach.

"The next time I call you, you better stop and see what I'm calling you for," the leader said. "Y'all come on. Plain Jane ain't as bad as we thought she was."

The excruciating pain ripped through my body as I slowly stood to my feet. I made it to my street and saw that my parents' car was not in the driveway. Feeling a slight sense of relief, I mustered up enough strength to make it inside the house and up to my room just in time. I remembered daddy's in-house remedy that he used whenever one of us had aches and pains in our body. Not wanting to have to answer any questions gave me just enough strength to make it back downstairs to retrieve the items I needed to soothe the pain. I made it back to my room without being seen. I settled into a hot, Epsom Salt bath and slowly replayed the brutal event. Flashes of blood invaded my mind.

The next morning, I returned to school and, to my surprise, there were pictures of what was supposed to be me posted on my locker, in the bathrooms, and throughout the hallways. The words 'Plain Jane' were written on each one in bold letters. For two long weeks, the British crew tortured me every chance they had—physically, mentally, and emotionally.

The day came when I woke up with vengeance weighing heavily on my heart. At school, I sat in the corner of the cafeteria eating my lunch while I kept a close watch on my tormentors. From my peripheral view, I watched as they moved closer and closer to where I sat.

"Why you sitting at our table?" asked the leader of the crew. She yanked my hair, almost causing me to fall away from the table. I reached for my tray of food—and then lost it! I beat her repeatedly with the empty tray as the other two girls watched in shock as the leader and I threw punches at each other. My opponent cried for her friends to assist her, but to my surprise, no one dared to intervene with what we had going on. Not long after, though, I felt someone grab me and start throwing blows to my head. I glanced and saw that the other two girls joined in on the attack. I refused to give up or give in. I had to come up with a plan fast! When I fell to the ground, that was my time to show out. I quickly reached inside my pocket, pulled out my secret weapon, and started stabbing my closest assailant.

I was frightened when I woke up six hours later in a hospital bed covered with bandages. My family sat at my bedside, and my room was filled with flowers. I tried to speak, but the pain I was in made it very difficult.

"Shhh, Baby; don't say anything," momma told me.

Daddy stood in the corner of the room praying and pleading the blood of Jesus over my life while Raven sat on the right side of my bed with what looked like the Bible opened as she read from Psalms.

The next day when the doctor came to check on me, he told me that it was by the grace of God that I was still alive because it obviously wasn't my time to go. *All these damn Jesus people… If he only knew the thoughts that were flooding my mind at that moment.*

Why didn't God just allow me to die?

"You're one lucky young lady. I'm telling you," the doctor mentioned.

"No, sir; she's not lucky. She's blessed." Momma corrected the doctor's choice of words.

For three days, I laid in the hospital bed unable to utter a word. When I was able to speak, momma gave me the run-down of what happened. I was cut across my neck and sliced from the corner of my right eye down to my chin. I received 30 stitches. Two of the girls were also in the hospital, but the leader of the trio had to be transported to another hospital. The staff claimed they wanted to keep the families apart. One of my attackers was upstairs in the Intensive Care Unit from a punctured lung. Nothing severe happened to my third opponent.

Every now and then, someone from the church would swing by. No one mentioned grandpa, and I never cared to ask about him. The doctor stated he wanted to keep me in the hospital for another week to monitor me and make sure I wouldn't catch an infection. When that week was up, I was released from the confines of that hospital bed.

The morning after my return home, I was surprised to hear my parents and the police downstairs discussing details of the fight. I almost pissed on myself when I heard the next words that were said by one of the officers: Even though I acted in self-defense, I would be arrested and charged with three counts of aggravated assault with a deadly weapon with the intent to kill and attempted murder. Daddy called me downstairs. I'd heard plenty of stories about how ice-cold the holding cells in the detention center are, so I made sure to dress accordingly.

Momma cried as the handcuffs were being placed on my wrists and I was led to the back of the police car. The detective handed daddy his business card, and I read his lips as he told daddy not to hesitate to call if he had any questions.

After my transport to the detention center, I was assessed hours later and finally able to make a phone call. Momma kept hollering about how God would fight this battle for me. I wasn't tryna hear that garbage. Where the hell was He all along? Probably sitting on His high chair staring into space. She went on to tell me that the families of the crew all pressed charges against me.

As soon as I walked inside the dorm, all eyes were glued on me. Some of the other girls kept whispering to each other. I kept my cool but wasn't about to be punked by some illegitimate females. I rolled my eyes at a few and kept moving, making my way to the cell I was assigned to. To my knowledge, the incident that went down at school was already the talk of the detention center. Some of the girls wanted to be down with me once we were released.

After one month of a thorough investigation, the charges against me were dismissed, except for the battery and aggravated assault with a deadly weapon with the intent to kill. Two of the three girls were later arrested with more serious charges, while the other member of the crew was still in the hospital with charges pending. Due to the nature of the case and the fact that a weapon was involved on the campus, I was sentenced to a level eight juvenile program for 18 months.

Chapter 15: Shanece
Forgiveness Broke the Stronghold

"So, this is where you been hiding out, huh, Ms. Holier-Than-Thou?" I stopped abruptly at the voice that addressed me.

"Well, hello to you, too," I said, facing the unwelcomed guest.

"You got jokes, huh? But I ain't come all the way down here for a show. You all grown up now. You done managed to get outta the ghetto, have kids, and looking hella fine, too. I never thought you had it in you. I know that people change, but I would never have thought God would have something to do with it."

"Well, thanks for the compliment. I see you done forgot whose bloodline I have pumping through my veins. I know times done changed, and we haven't seen each other in some years, but I'm still the same Nece," I said, tryna keep the visit on a good note since my daughter was accompanying me.

"Momma, I know him."

"Baby, be quiet."

Already tired of his nonsense, I inquired, "What can I do for you today?"

"You can do a lot for me right about now, but for starters, you can go ahead and put your daughter in the car."

"You can't be serious. She's not going anywhere without me."

"Alright. Alright. Since you wanna act tough, I have no objection to that. I do need to holla at you about something, though."

"We have nothing to talk about."

"Woman, what you mean? We have a lot of catching up to do. My daughter is locked up behind some mess, and these people talking 'bout charging my baby as an adult."

My head was starting to spin. It was all making sense now. It's no wonder why the hospital thought it would be best to keep the families separated. Tryna play it cool, I responded, "And you're saying this to say what?"

"Girl, what part of what I said ain't you comprehending? Read between the lines. I know you ain't no dummy 'cause hell, you managed to escape my hands. Man, here go a few dollars. Take this money. I just need you to drop the charges."

"You're one pathetic son of a b***h. You had the nerve to show up at my church with this nonsense? Tryna extort me? Have you ever thought about apologizing to me for what you've done to me?"

"Apologize to you for what? Huh? For being a crackhead like your ol' base-head momma? Apologize for teaching you to be good at what you do best, just like your whoring momma? Huh? Tell me, 'cause the last time I checked, I did both y'all a favor."

"You did us a favor? Is that what you call 'favor'? Stealing my vir…" I managed to stop midtrack before I spilled the beans about the truth of my past that I've been hiding my entire life. If my daughters were to ever learn about the real me, I don't think I'll be able to forgive myself.

"Listen, Nece: Stop running from your past and face it. Don't forget who held you down when no one else wanted you. It was me! I was the one who stood up and took that spot."

"You should have left me in the system. I probably would have had a better life. But you know what? You're absolutely right about all that you just said. It would have been better if you wouldn't have done none of what you did. And trust: I appreciate you for making sure I had a roof over my head and food to eat. But you see, because I'm a changed person and now have the love of God flowing through my heart, I'm able to look you in the face and have this conversation. Not only that, I'm able to let you know that you don't have to apologize to me. I forgive you for every damage, hurt, and pain you've caused me. Everything happened for a reason, and I trust that God is gonna continue to use my brokenness as one of His strong vessels. Now, have a nice life."

Before more damage was done, I reached for Raven's hand and led her away, leaving Uncle Dean standing in that same spot looking shocked and speechless.

Chapter 16: Raven
Forgiveness: It's for Me

I can't seem to understand what went wrong with momma, but ever since we saw Timeless last week, she's been acting strange, 'round here looking like the walking dead. She wasn't acting like her usual self, and all her conversations consisted of one-word responses. When I questioned daddy about her unusual behavior, he brushed it off like it's nothing, telling me to just pray for her.

"Momma, are we going to Bible study tonight?"

"Yes," she replied while staring blankly at me.

"What's wrong with you, momma? Lately, you've been looking zoned out, as if something is seriously wrong with you."

Ignoring my question, she sat still in the chair and continued looking at me with bloodshot eyes bulging from her head and sweating profusely.

"Hello, momma? I'm talking to you. And why are you sweating like that?" I asked, feeling both sorry and disgusted at the same time. "Okay, momma; I guess I'm talking to myself, so I'll see you later at Bible study." Leaving her alone, I raced upstairs to my bedroom. My mind wandered to thoughts of my sister. Since she'd left, I hadn't been able to visit her. I pray that God would allow this circumstance to be a wake-up call for her and, in the end, it will be used to glorify God.

On our way to Bible study, I sat nervously in the back seat of the car with thoughts of what must be done tonight. Different ideas came to my mind on how I should accomplish my plan, but those thoughts were soon erased and replaced with the 'whys' and the 'what ifs.' Momma was unable to join us tonight, so daddy and I entered the sanctuary together. *There aren't too many people in the house tonight*, I thought while I scanned the sanctuary searching for any familiar faces who decided to show up tonight. Daddy took his seat in the front row while I sat tucked off towards the back. I listened carefully as Minister Sonia stood behind the pulpit pouring out her heart. Everyone ain't able, but God sure has blessed Minister Sonia with a beautiful voice that she used to glorify Him—and she sure knows how to gain the attention of her audience with the awesome teaching she was now sharing.

"When I grow up, I wanna be just like Minister Sonia," I mumbled to myself. No one knows it, but from the first time I met Minister Sonia, I've looked up to her. Her appearance, the way she carries herself, her love for the Lord, and doing a great work for the Lord are all the great qualities I've always admired most about her. Tonight, she was preaching on the topic of putting patience to work. That's something that I lack, but one that is a critical factor in my walk with Christ.

Forty-five minutes into the teaching, I saw him stand and exit through the door to the cafeteria. Minutes later, I was able to sneak out behind him unnoticed. When I reached the cafeteria, I saw him pour a cup of coffee. I watched him as he sat down with his back facing me. Fear took me by surprise and sweat began to settle in on my forehead. At that moment, I wanted to run, but it was too late. It was either now or never. I hadn't come this far to turn back.

I quietly approached him and stood next to where he was seated. "Excuse me," I said, interrupting whatever it was that weighed heavily on his mind. My sudden presence caused him to spill the contents that filled his cup.

Standing and nervously looking around, he asked, "What are you doing in here?"

"I came to talk to you."

"You came in here to talk to me about what?" was his nervous response. He continued glancing over his should every few seconds. "Who knows you're in here?"

"Listen: No one knows about me being here. I actually came on my own to talk to you."

"I wanna know who the hell sent you? That's what I wanna know." Paranoia overtook him as he rambled on and on about nothing that made sense.

"Can I talk now or are you gonna stand here and continue running your mouth?"

"Lil girl, don't you know to have some manners? I'm still your…"

I cut him off. "This won't take long. I promise. I came here because I am ready to let go of the past and move forward with my life. I didn't come here to know why you did what you did or to get an apology from you 'cause most likely, I'm not gonna receive one. But I did come to let you know that even after everything you have done to me, I still love you. I forgive you as well. I forgive you for all the times you've hurt me and the pain you've caused in my life."

Looking at me awkwardly and continuously shifting his weight from one foot to the next, he asked in disbelief, "You forgive who? Me? And what made you wanna do that?"

"Jesus. He is the reason behind my decision. This has nothing to do with you. I'm doing it for me, to free myself from any stronghold against me—whether it's anger or any other form of hatred that I once held towards you."

In that minute, I felt a strange feeling. It was a sense of relief that came upon me as those words departed my lips. With that, I politely walked away and rejoined everyone just as they gathered together to say a word of prayer. Once I reached home and settled in my bed, I happened to get a word from the Lord as I opened my Bible and came upon Deuteronomy 28. The scripture was titled "Blessings for Obedience." Verses 1-14 were clearly directed towards me.

The following Sunday after church, I was baptized. While I was coming up from under the water, I felt my body tremble. As I opened my eyes, there stood an angel before me. Daddy must have seen her, too, because he looked at me and smiled as he whispered in my ear, "God is very pleased with you today."

Chapter 17: Shanece
My Choices: My Consequence

Moving from Coral Springs, where I was raised, to Coconut Creek was useless. News travels fast. You can pay a crackhead five dollars, and they'll give you all the business. Timeless' wife is the owner of the salon where I get my hair and nails done, and she doesn't know how to keep her mouth shut. A person like that can't be trusted. If it were her choice, she'd tell you all her man's business. It surprised me when I found out they were married. She enjoys flaunting her lavish life and bragging about how much money Timeless has. Week after week, whenever I would visit the shop, the bulk of her conversations were mainly about Timeless. It didn't amaze me how all the clients sat there listening with jealousy, lusting after her riches and fame. She must not have realized each was waiting in line for the opportunity to claim Wifey's throne.

I must give credit when credit is due. The girl can do some hair. I'll give her that much. There's no doubt about that, so she used that to her advantage by making sure her clients pay 10% upfront every time they book an appointment. She also charges an extra $15.00 for being late and $25.00 for a no-show. Not to mention my nail tech. She is bad at what she does—and that's bad in the best way.

That's why you can catch me at the salon week after week, soaking up all the drama.

Thanks to Bre', without me asking, she voluntarily gave me the "T": After Timeless was released from prison, he went back into the drug game and was now running things. Growing up, momma would always harass him about when he gon' have a baby, and it never failed. His answer would always be the same at the end of every conversation, so I found it hard to believe the day Bre' spilled the beans and told everyone that her title is not just Wifey, but he was also the father of their daughter. I still had doubts in my mind until the day I sat under the dryer and saw Timeless and the little girl walk through the door carrying a bag with what looked like a plate of food in her little hands.

Hell, I nearly screamed! I had to use the magazine I was reading to hide my face. Curiosity had the best of me, though. Every so often, I would peek and watch as the couple exchanged a few words, hugs, then a goodbye kiss. That five-minute moment erased all doubts I once had after I realized that Timeless and the little girl could be twins. She had his high-yellow complexion and high cheekbones. The high cheekbones were something we inherited from the maternal side of the family.

After momma was sent to prison, no one knew the things I had to do to survive in the streets. No one knew of my secrets. I buried that side of my life the day I said: "I do." Now, I feel trapped with my past lingering over my head. It's finally catching up to me. Now I have Timeless tracking my every move and threatening to disclose all my dirty laundry secrets if I don't make a move about the pending charges against his daughter.

I was stressed out and under pressure. At night, I found myself spending hours awake, drenched in sweat from the ongoing nightmares of someone trying to kill me. My husband did everything he could to help, but I just wanted to be left alone. To his surprise, in time, I stopped visiting my therapist and going to church. They were of no use. The consequence of my choices is that I'm back strung out on drugs. Hell, I even breathe the feeling of having the taste in my mouth.

That is what I live to do—not be some damn pastor's wife.

Chapter 18: Kelis
Fifty-Six…and Counting

Being in the program wasn't as bad as I thought it would be. My first month here, I was constantly being tossed in isolation from being involved in fights with the other girls. When I first got here, everyone already knew who I was before I even arrived. In fact, they were expecting my arrival. Every girl in here belongs to a clique of some sort. I, on the other hand, stayed to myself. My last fight didn't go so well. What was supposed to be a one-on-one fair fight turned into a riot that resulted in a staff member breaking her leg and another getting the palm of her hand sliced open when she reached for the blade. Her Superwoman stunt actually saved a girl from getting cut up. There were 20 girls involved in the riot, including me. All of us were transported throughout Florida to different programs with added charges, except for three of the girls who just so happened to be at the wrong place at the wrong time.

Momma stopped coming to visitation almost a year ago. Daddy never missed a visit. He faithfully made it here every weekend, and every time he came, he brought the Bible along with him. During the six hours he visited me, I would normally sit and tune him out while he ranted about how important it is to involve God in my everyday life. Raven has never come to visit me. Her excuse was that she couldn't stand seeing me this way, but she made sure to keep me updated on what's happening on the outside by sending letters and pictures. We often spoke on the telephone on Thursdays when I would get my free phone call for the week. Besides daddy, she was the only access I had to life outside these walls. I made sure to stress the fact that I still wasn't interested in hearing anything about God or His Son. I wasn't at all surprised when Raven broke the news by telling me how she got baptized. I wouldn't put it past her. She is, after all, a Jesus Freak. I just don't understand how she can love someone she ain't never met.

"Okay, girllll! You ain't got nothing else to talk about besides all this? I don't care nothing 'bout you seeing no damn angel. You're delusional. Them things ain't even real," I said, irritated as she rambled on and on about the day of her baptism.

"You're being so selfish right about now."

"How the hell I'm being selfish? Stop using words you don't know the exact definition of. Selfish is you forcing your false religion on me. I already told you I couldn't care less about Jesus and all those lies you keep telling me about what He done did. Tell me: Who can really turn water into wine and feed all those damn people with only five loaves of bread and two fish? Is He some type of magician or something? If He's so real and cares so much, tell Him to get me up outta here and, while you're doing that, ask Him where the hell He was while I was being bullied and damn near lost my life? Ain't He supposed to be there protecting us—His kids?"

"He ain't let you die, did He? Okay, then. And, by the way, you become one of His when you accept Him, and you're saved."

"He might as well had let them kill me. My miseries would have been over with. I wouldn't be here right now having this conversation with you. Now, with that being said, I only have ten more minutes to be on the phone, and I'm through with this Jesus talk. So, tell me what else been going on out there? Any new drama?"

"That's all you wanna hear about, with your messy self."

"Yeah, and you're right along with me, church girl!"

"Anyways, I ain't got no more "T" for you. Oh! Yes, I do! How about I was eavesdropping on daddy having a conversation with your lawyer the other day, and he was talking about how the case against Rihanna was dropped to a lesser charge and how she gotta do three years in a program. So, yeah: She gon' be right there with you. You might even see her."

"I doubt they'll be that dumb and send her here, but okay…if you think so."

"Daddy went on to say that he thinks Timeless paid off the prosecutor."

"Umm, yeah: I would think so, too. With all the money he has, ain't no telling who else he done paid off. I don't put nothing past him. If they know like I know, this beef ain't over with. They better not send Rihanna nowhere close to where I'm at!"

"Girl, if they do, you better not do nothing crazy 'cause you 'bout to come home. You know we can't have you catching no extra charges. Plus, you and I have a lot of catching up to do!"

"As long as our catching up doesn't include God, you can count me in."

"I guess I need to go ahead and find another sister then 'cause Baby, God is included in everything I do!"

"Get your search on then. Anyways, I have to go now. This lady keeps looking at me all crazy and trust when I say I don't wanna have to lose my phone privileges. I'll talk to you next week, same time. I love you, girl."

"I love you more, Sissy."

I returned to my room, took out my calendar, and started counting off my days—something I've been doing since the first day I was arrested. Fifty-six days to go before I'm able to get a taste of freedom.

Chapter 19: Raven
Momma's Sudden Departure

Kelis didn't know it, but I was already making plans for the two of us. Our church will be conducting rehearsals for the pageant show this Christmas—the week of her return home—and I wanted us to partake and be among its contestants. I was also thinking of a welcome home party for her, but first, I needed to get my parents' approval.

I arrived home late from my soccer game and made a beeline for the kitchen to help myself to something to eat. Excited about sharing my good news with everyone, I gulped down the remainder of the Kool-Aid and pulled out my report card from my backpack. Feeling proud of myself, I smiled again knowing that once again, my report card was cheesing with all "As." That was something my parents loved about me. I took pride in my grades. I've never received a grade below an "A."

Momma's car was parked In the driveway, so I took that as a sign that she was home. "Mom…Mommy! Mom! Where are you?" I called out.

After looking around downstairs, I climbed the stairs to her bedroom. The door was closed. Momma doesn't like uninvited guests, so I knocked on the door and called her name. I didn't get a reply. Still holding on to my report card in one hand, I reached for the doorknob with the other. I opened the door and invited myself in. My excitement was bubbling over!

"Mommy, are you in here?" I asked, looking around the room for her. "I have something to show you!" I said. When I opened her closet, I nearly collapsed at the sight before me. Tears filled my eyes as I looked down at my momma. She was half-naked and barely propped up against the wall. There was a needle in her arm, and a slew of empty pill bottles lay before her.

Fifteen minutes later, our house was labeled a crime scene. Police filled the inside of our home. They were taking pictures and asking questions that neither daddy nor I wanted to be bothered with. The detective got the message, gave his card to daddy, and told daddy if he thinks of anything that can help with their investigation to feel free to give him a call. He then politely excused himself. Daddy was crying so hard, the police kept asking him if he had any intentions on hurting himself or someone else.

"For the last time, I said no! Please stop asking me unnecessary questions!" daddy barked at the annoying cop.

"I'm sorry, sir, about your loss, but these are necessary precaution questions we have to ask. Here's a card for the suicide prevention team. If you have any questions or need someone to talk to, don't hesitate to either give them a call or you can reach me on my cell."

All the neighbors were gathered outside, acting concerned and asking the emergency personnel what had happened. In all actuality, they wanted to be nosy. Just as I was about to open my mouth, I stopped and watched my momma being carried out on the stretcher wrapped in a body bag. After it was safe to re-enter our house, I went to my room and gave daddy some space while he stayed downstairs and bawled his heart out.

Days after momma's death, with the help of our church family, daddy was finally able to pull himself together and start to make the funeral arrangements. He was fortunate enough to pull some strings for Kelis to be released a week early, which was the week of our mother's funeral.

I decided to drive the four-hour ride with daddy to get Kelis from the program. When we got there, she was filled with excitement about coming home early. I helped her load all her belongings into the car as she talked my ears off about a fight she recently got into.

"Umm…hello? Why am I the only one happy in this car? What's going on? Y'all ain't happy to see me? Oh! I forgot to add FINALLY in that sentence. Yes, I'm FINALLY home—and a week early, at that!"

"No, Sis; please don't take it personally. It's not that," I said.

"Then, what is it?" she asked, interrupting my thoughts as I tried to think of something to take her focus away from me. "Girl, I'm talking to you! Answer me!" Kelis' demand sliced through the quiet of the car as I prepared to share with her the news. Actually, I didn't wanna be the one to deliver the sad news.

"I just have a lot on my mind. That's all," I said.

"Nah. Something ain't right. What the hell happened?"

"Kelis. Baby, something bad happened," Daddy said.

"Yeah, that's every day in my world. Tell me something new, daddy."

"Well, daughter, in this case, it's different. I don't know how to tell you this, but…" Daddy's voice trailed off. He pulled the car over, put it in park, and broke down crying again.

"Daddy, please. Just stop and tell me what's going on! I hate to be the last one to find out about stuff."

"Baby, she's gone. I'm sorry, but she's gone. I did everything I could, but I just couldn't save her."

"Who, daddy? Who's gone, daddy?"

He continued to cry uncontrollably.

"Daddy, answer me! WHO'S GONE?" The panic was evident.

"Your momma…she's gone."

"What are you talking 'bout? She's gone? Gone where?"

"Your…momma…is…dead, Baby."

"Noooooo! This can't be! Noooooo!" Kelis squealed. "Daddy, please tell me you're lying. Raven, tell me he's lying. TELL ME, DAMNIT! Daddy! Somebody, answer me! Where's momma?" She began to scream again, grabbing my arms and shaking me.

I shook my head, giving her an answer she wasn't expecting— an answer even I had yet to accept. I know that my sister was hurting. She and momma have always been very close. Daddy was my favorite. Kelis threw punches at me while I tried my best to console her. She was in complete hysterics.

"Get away from me! Y'all and all this Jesus mess! What you gonna tell me now? That God loves me, huh? I don't wanna hear it. He took my momma away from me! He's supposed to be God, right? So, He knows how much I love her. He knows how much she meant to me, yet He took her away? Why? Tell me why! Why God had to do that to me? Why He have to take her? Momma ain't here no more. What I'm gonna do? Ohhhh nooooo! I can't do this! I can't believe He took her from me. She was the one person on this earth who understands me!"

For the remainder of the ride home, I embraced my twin, and we cried together.

The rest of the week went by pretty fast. Momma went out in style. Daddy made sure of that. The First Baptist Church of Christ was filled with its usual array of faces and a few unknown visitors. It was hectic all morning. In all the years I've been a member, I've never witnessed First Baptist as crowded as it was that day. It was so crowded, people had to stand alongside the walls. Minister Sonia sang a solo and daddy did the honors by sending momma home with best wishes.

After everything was all said and done, we headed to the graveyard to say our last goodbyes while momma was being lowered into the ground. Timeless approached us and addressed daddy, handing him a manila envelope. I was surprised that he came through to pay his respects, especially after the last heated encounter he had with momma outside the church house.

"What's this?" daddy asked in between sobs. Timeless held out his hand, waiting for daddy to acknowledge it for a handshake.

"That's just a lil something for the girls. Boss, I'm sorry for your loss. She was family to me, too, so I understand how you feel. The least I can do is look out for the girls."

All of us eyed him with curiosity after the words *"She was family to me"* left his mouth.

Daddy accepted Timeless' kind gesture. They shook hands, and the men went their separate ways.

Chapter 20: Kelis
The "Timeless" Act of Betrayal

A few days after the funeral, I was digging through momma's closet and located her journal. Reading through it word-for-word, I discovered all the hidden secrets about Timeless. It all made sense as to why he handed daddy the manila envelope that was filled with cash. He was the main reason behind her death and considered us to be charity. He felt obligated. I felt totally disgusted at the thought of Timeless taking advantage of momma—not to mention the one part that stood out the most to me: picturing Timeless as he sat back and watched while his boys took their turns satisfying their sickening desire for a child. My blood started boiling. I was very angry at Timeless by his act of betrayal. My desire to pay him back for all the pains and hurt he inflicted on my momma was strong.

After momma's death, my family took a drastic turn. Daddy had to step down from his pastoral position. He started not being around as much at home. Most of his time was spent at a nearby bar as he drank his life away. I teamed up with a group of girls from Lauderhill who welcomed and accepted me as family. The oldest of the group was three years older than me. Her name was Zariah (they called her Zari), and she was a 16-year-old Jamaican native. Zari was fully-grown in her own way. She had a boyfriend named Blaze whom she claimed took her virginity. Blaze is a 19-year-old nickel-and-dime petty hustler who spent most of his days in the streets tryna make a name for himself.

Zari introduced me to boosting. Every day after school, she would pick me up in Blaze's truck, and the four of us would hit up a few stores inside the mall. Thanks to Zari for putting me on 'cause my wardrobe was lit! In school, I was everyone's crush.

"Where are you coming from at this time of night?" Raven asked while blocking me from entering the house.

"So, what? You my momma now?"

"Who tryna be your momma? Lately, you been coming home at these crazy hours like you grown."

"I'm grown enough to stand on my own two feet. Now, get outta my way!"

"I just want the best for you, Sis."

"Girl, my momma is dead. Stop tryna do what she didn't!"

"How dare you say something like that about her!" Raven yelled.

Turning around, I responded, "If you want the best for me, start by finding you some damn business and stay outta mines!" I stormed up the stairs with my bags in hand and slammed the door. Putting my shopping bags on the bed, I took out my stash and lit up a blunt, getting my smoke on. Laying down on the bed, I tried gathering my thoughts as I replayed the words Raven said to me. I knew I had said some hurtful words, but it was too late; the damage was done.

The next day after school, we went out boosting so I could get some things for Raven. The minute we walked inside the store, my stomach decided it wanted to make noises—the same funny noise it would make whenever I would get nervous about something.

"Girl, why you keep looking like that?" Zari asked.

"My bad, but I'm really not feeling good."

"Ahhh! Don't tell me you scared now?"

"I don't know what it is, but something ain't sitting right with me."

"Man, if you don't get outta here with that. You straight bugging for real! I'm 'bout to go over here and get me one of those dresses I saw on the web earlier."

"Do your thing. I'll be outside waiting on y'all."

Forty-five minutes into my wait, two police pulled up, got outta their cars, and entered the same store my girls were in. Not too long after, the girls were being escorted out and placed in the back of separate cars. Blaze gave me a ride home.

When I arrived, Raven was sitting down at the dining room table with her Bible opened in front of her.

"What's this?" she asked as I placed the bag of clothes on the table.

"Just some stuff I got you."

"You don't have a job, so where you got the money to buy this type of stuff?"

"I didn't. Someone bought it for me."

"You must think I'm dumb! Nice try, though. I don't want it. I don't want no part in whatever you got going on."

"Come on, Raven. Please. Just take it."

"Girl, I said no! Take them back to the store or back to whoever bought it for you so y'all can get your money back."

Zariah called me the following day. Since it was her first time getting caught, she was fortunate enough to be released on her own recognizance. She was ordered to stay away from that store. The other two girls weren't as lucky.

Chapter 21: Raven
Tragedy Strikes Twice

The banging noise startled me out of my sleep. I glanced at the clock that read 2:00. Whoever it is knocking at the door can't be in their right mind showing up at this time of the morning. Peeping through the window, there were three cars parked in front of the house. One, in particular, stood out to me.

"I'm coming," I yelled while making my way to the door.

"Yes, how may I help you?" I said as I slung the door wide open.

"I'm sorry Kel…" There stood some strangers at the door with my grandpa lingering in the background.

"Kelis isn't here right now. Is this visit about her?" I asked, feeling irritated as I tried wiping the sleep from my eyes.

"No, it's not about her. Do you mind if we come in?"

"First, tell me what it's about. I can't just invite you in, and I don't know what you're here for."

"Trust me. I understand, but it would be better if we came in."

"I guess. Come on in." Grandpa introduced the lady as a representative from Child Protective Services. It was the police officer who gave me the rundown for the reason of their late-hour visit.

Once again, daddy had been drinking and driving and was on his way home from the casino—only this time, his truck collided with another car. The driver of the other car was seven months pregnant and had her two-year-old son with her in the back seat who died on the scene. The lady was rushed to the hospital. She survived, but her unborn didn't make it.

I jumped up from my seat and turned the television on just in time. The accident was being reported live as breaking news.

Daddy was being charged with double homicide, vehicular manslaughter, and reckless driving. His alcohol level was .60, higher than what's allowed under Florida law.

"I'm very sorry, Raven. I know you just lost your mother a year ago, and now this. It's yet another horrible tragedy," said the CPS representative. "But I want you to know that we're here to help. Your father advised us that both you and your sister would be here. That's why we came now."

"So, what's gonna happen now? I mean, with my sister and me?"

"Normally, in a situation like this, we would take into our custody any children in the home, especially if there are no close relatives to take charge, until we're either able to find a home or close family member who's willing to take custody. However, in your case, as you can see, your grandfather is here with us, so I'm going to recommend temporary custody to him until we know the full extent of your father's case. Then, we will go from there."

"So, you're tryna tell me that we have to move in with him or will we be able to stay living in our own house?"

"No, my dear: You girls will be moving in with him. By the way, where's your sister?"

"I don't know where she…" I started to say, just as Kelis walked through the door.

"What all these people doing in here?"

Everyone introduced themselves. This time, the CPS representative told Kelis about daddy's tragedy. By the time she was through, Kelis was having a fit when she realized we would be moving in with grandpa.

"Y'all can miss me with all that. Ain't no damn way I'm moving into his house. You can just forget that. I refuse to move in with the devil himself!"

"You only have two choices here: Either you move in with him, or you can just pack your things and come with me. We'll find someone who's willing to adopt you or, better yet, you can go to one of our group homes."

"You must be outta your mind! Do I look homeless? Ain't nobody adopting me and I damn sure ain't going to no damn group home. I don't see why the hell I need to be living with someone else when I'm perfectly fine right where I am!"

"Like I said, young lady: Because y'all are minors and can't live here by yourself without an adult in the house."

"What, lady? What you talking 'bout? You must ain't know. We are grown! We don't need no more adults here. We good. We can handle this here on our own."

"Lil girl, I'm not doing this with you. So, what you wanna do? You wanna go stay with your grandfather? If not, you're going to come with me, and we'll find a home for you."

"So, besides another family member, he's our only option?"

"Yes, he is."

"Nah. I'm good. I guess I'll go with him."

Chapter 22: Raven
I Could Have Let Him Die

The news media had a field day painting a horrific image of the type of person daddy is. Everyone was astonished when it was revealed that he was once part of a Ponzi scheme back in the day, way before he decided to give his life to Jesus. All the good he had once done for the community was quickly forgotten. All ears were focused solely on his past and the crimes he had committed.

For two years, our family was dragged and tossed through the embarrassment and shame we received from the members at First Baptist Church of Christ once the dark secrets of our parents' lives were exposed. By the time we turned 16, the scars that were left behind were beyond healing. Daddy was caught up in a win-lose situation. He could take the case to trial, but with all the evidence they had against him, he'd be blessed if they didn't hit him with the death penalty—which is what the prosecution was aiming for.

With all the prayers and fasting daddy was doing behind bars, God showed him favor when his attorney returned and gave us the news that the State's Attorney agreed to a 15-year prison sentence. That meant he'd be 54 the next time he's able to have a chance to see his freedom again. At the sentencing, with hardcore tears in his eyes, he sincerely apologized to the family and us for failing us and dragging our lives into his mess. When it was my time to speak, I broke down.

"Daddy, you were a great father and, even though this happened, you still are. You took care of us, and I always thank God for having a father like you. Continue to trust in the Lord and in all your ways, acknowledge and trust Him. Daddy, I love you. I always will." In response, he told me that he loves me as well. "I also would like to say to the family that I am truly sorry for your loss. I truly wish I can take back all the pain and tears this situation has caused."

Kelis declined to take the stand. Grandpa promised daddy that he would do the best he can to take care of us. He kept that promise until the day after court when the deputy hauled daddy away, and he started making death threats to keep me silent when daddy called or our social worker stopped by to visit us.

The abuse grew more gruesome over the years. Grandpa started acting and treating me as if we were a couple. After CPS closed the case, he turned me into his house slave. Before I left for school in the morning, I had to get up early to cook his breakfast. Dinner had to be ready before 6:00 p.m. sharp. The house had to be kept clean at all times, not to mention folding his clothes and them being properly ironed. He even went as far as to make extra space in his closet for my clothes and forced me to share his bedroom with him. That way, he would have easy access to my body as he would like. Kelis was my only escape. She was rarely home, but when she was, I was allowed to sleep in my own room. The thought of losing my sister to the angel of death because of me put genuine fear in my heart.

As the days passed, outta nowhere, grandpa became very ill. With the hope of a future, I managed to get a job as a cashier at a nearby grocery store. I came home from work a little past noon one day, just in time to hear the sound of his groaning voice coming from his bedroom. When I got to the door of his room, I found him lying flat on his back with one hand resting on his chest. I rolled my eyes and turned to leave when I felt a sudden change as the Holy Spirit took over. I obeyed as He spoke to me:

"Love your enemies. Do good to those who hate you. Bless those who curse you and pray for those who mistreat you."

The last part was what stood out the most as I picked up the phone, dialed 911, and spoke to the operator as I gave our exact location.

Then, I did as the Lord instructed me to do: I prayed.

"Heavenly Father, I'm coming to You this day in humbleness and meekness, in the name of my Lord and Savior. Lord, I lift up to You my grandpa. I'm asking that You please forgive both of us for our sins, known and unknown. Wash them, and they'll be whiter than snow. Cleanse us from all unrighteousness and create in us a new heart, O God, and renew a steadfast spirit in us. Father, bless him, watch over him, and protect him from any harm or danger. I'm asking that You send many of Your angels to be his rearward guard. If he stumbles, they will catch him. Whatever it is that is going on with him, I'm asking that You heal him for Your name's sake, and he will glorify Your name.

"Father, give him grace and mercy. I'm asking that You answer my prayer according to Your love and kindness. Heavenly Father, I declare Your faithfulness to the heavens that by the stripes of Your Son, Jesus Christ, grandpa is healed. In Jesus' name, I pray, Amen."

Soon after opening my eyes, there was a knock on the door. The paramedics did a brief assessment of grandpa's health, placed him in the ambulance, and rushed him to the hospital with lights and sirens blaring.

Chapter 23: Raven
Touch NOT My Anointed!

"May I speak with Ms. Raven, please?"

"This is her. How may I help you?"

"My name is Doctor Pulaski. Your information is listed here as an emergency contact for your grandfather, Mr. Jones."

I wondered when and how that happened...

"Hello? Are you there?"

"Yes, I'm still here. Sorry about that."

"As I was mentioning, ma'am, I am calling to give you an update of his health status. Within the 24-hour timeframe that he's been admitted, he has already had two heart attacks. His heart isn't looking too great at this time. It's functioning at 17% of what a normal heart should."

"I don't understand all that medical terminology, so can you please give me a simpler breakdown of what you're saying to me?"

"Most definitely." I could tell the doctor was used to that type of question as he proceeded. "Basically, what that means is that his heart is failing. We're going to have to conduct open-heart surgery. However, I'm afraid to say that if we do the surgery, there's a 95% chance he will not survive."

Cutting him off, I said, "Ummm, excuse me, Doctor…?"

"Doctor Pulaski."

"Yes. Doctor Pulaski. I have to let you know that my grandfather will not be needing open-heart surgery. As a matter-of-fact, you nor no one on your staff better not lay a finger on him. My Father is going to heal him."

"I'm sorry. Your who?"

"You heard me correctly. I said my Father."

"And whom might that be?"

"That person would be God."

"Oh boy. Another one of them," he muttered.

I heard the doctor's sarcastic remark and replied, "Excuse me?!"

"I'm sorry. I wasn't speaking to you."

Liar. I brushed it off and continued. "If you don't mind me getting back to what I was saying; I'll be there tomorrow around this time and, by the way, Doc: Thank you very much for calling."

Ending the call, instead of going to lunch, I diverted my attention to the library where I began my 30-minute prayer, read a few scriptures from the Bible, and then was led into a 24-hour fast.

During my walk with the Lord, I've often read in the Bible about Jesus performing miraculous healings according to His Word. He has given to us—the ones who are His own—the authority to drive out impure spirits and heal every disease and sickness. The words of God are still alive to this day, just as they were back then. I am a child of the Most High God, for I am born again of the incorruptible seed of the Word of God and redeemed from the curse of the law of sin and death.

Chapter 24: Kelis
Truths Exposed

"For the last time: HELLO? Who's this?"

"Oh. My bad. Wassup?" Raven replied.

"Girl, why you ain't said nothing?"

"Dang, I said my bad. I ain't know you had picked up."

"Well, duh! I been on the phone saying 'hello' for the longest and you weren't saying nothing."

"Wassup with all that noise in the background? What you got going on over there?"

"Getting ready to smoke me some of this good Jamaican ganja I just finished rollin'."

"I'm still praying for you, Sis. I hope that you'll come around one day."

"Oh, hell nah! There you go with that Jesus mess again. Man, how many times I done told you to keep that kind of talking to yourself, bruh? Like straight up: You starting to get on my nerves. I don't care for the Man, so stop bringing Him up. What part of that don't you understand? Besides, what's the real reason you called? Once I start smoking, I don't need you messing up my high."

"Why you didn't return my call earlier?"

"Wait. Wait. Wait. Who the hell you call yourself checking? Don't forget: I am older than you!"

"What? By a few seconds? That don't count."

"Actually, Kelis, it's by a few minutes, so it does count. I can't believe this is what you were really tryna get a hold of me for. You really tryna blow my high with all this damn interrogating!"

"That's not all I called you for. Grandpa is in the hospital." I could hear a pin drop…in China.

Kelis' response came back with a venomous sting. "Girl, I almost hung up on you. What you telling me that for?"

"Because you need to know! He went in last night. The doctor just called a few minutes ago talking 'bout things ain't looking too good for him."

"And, again: You're calling to tell me this for what reason?"

"What you mean 'for what reason'? We should go see him. I'm going up there tomorrow after school. You should just come with me."

"You lucky you my sister 'cause I almost told you something about yourself. Listen to what I have to say and listen very closely:

That bastard ain't related to me. He might be some kin to you, but he damn sure don't mean nothing to me. Now, if you wanna be dumb and go see him, then that's on you. But me? I ain't stepping nowhere near no hospital. How I look going to see about a nigga who can't stand the ground I walk on, much less stand me? Oh, by the way, did you know that son of a…"

"Girl! Please have some respect and watch your mouth when you talk to me!" I had to calm her down. This conversation was getting heated. What had Kelis' panties all in a bunch, I wondered.

"I ain't even much paying you no attention. You don't own me, so let's first get that fact straight. Back to what I was saying. Did you know the son of a…you know what? I'll just call him a shriveled-up bastard. Do you know what he had the nerve to tell me the other day when I came by the house to get the rest of my stuff? That he couldn't stand momma, talking 'bout how he told daddy not to marry her and that when we were born and he saw that I looked just like her, he immediately hated me; but the minute he saw you, he loved you 'cause you was the exact image of daddy. He telling me that like I asked to be born into this damn dysfunctional family. The sad part is the man probably didn't even know my name yet. I spent the next hour releasing the anger I always felt toward the man I once looked up to as my grandpa. I have waited patiently for this day to finally arrive. I knew it was coming.

"Raven, I love you and all, Sis, but the next time you wanna call me about him, just make sure you're calling to ask for my address to send me an invitation to his funeral. When he dies, I don't wanna hear the news from word of mouth. I wanna be there to see for myself that yes, it is truly him finally getting buried so I can gag and spit on his casket."

Feeling relieved after finally releasing a bit of my frustration, I quickly ended the call before Raven could respond and powered off my phone. I didn't want to be bothered during my recreation time.

Chapter 25: Raven
Life-Changing Prayers

I stood at grandpa's bedside with my Bible open before me. Before I could utter a word, Doctor Pulaski's unannounced presence interrupted my peaceful thoughts. "The nurse mentioned to me that you were here again. I'm Doctor Pulaski. It's nice to finally meet you."

"Thank you. Nice to meet you as well."

"I'm glad you were able to make it in today, despite that you denied having us move forward with the procedure. However, we did run a few new tests on him. After reading the results, it's showing that he has a blockage in his heart that is slowing the blood process from freely flowing. We might have a chance of saving his life but to be sure, we must act fast and conduct surgery."

"Thank you for your concern, Doctor. Surgery will not be necessary."

"I'm afraid I'm not comprehending what you're saying."

"Let me ask you a question: You don't believe in God, do you?"

"What my beliefs are have nothing to do with what we're talking about."

"They have everything to do with it because I believe in Him—the Creator of you and me—and when my grandfather first wasn't feeling well, He wouldn't have told me to lay hands on him. Also, He wouldn't have sent me here if He knew a miracle wasn't about to take place."

"Wow, young lady. You're talking recklessly and too fast. Tell me again who's supposed to be the one healing him?"

"The Almighty God that I serve is able to do exceedingly abundantly beyond what you or I can imagine or ask for."

"I'm very curious to know: How is it that this 'God' will be doing something like that when He's not here with us?"

"If only you know what I know. His presence is in this room right now as we speak."

"I think you're losing it, Ms. Raven. So, just in case this 'God' doesn't show up, just have one of the nurses give me a call." Doctor Pulaski walked away mumbling something under his breath. It sounded to me like that same comment he made on the phone yesterday.

I believe that whatever I ask Jesus for in prayer, He will give it to me. Knowing that He didn't bring me this far to let me down, I closed the door to my grandpa's room then silently prayed for myself. When I was done praying, I located the story about Jesus healing the sick woman in the Bible. God specifically directed me to read verses forty-three through fifty-five. I started to feel relaxed, and a warm feeling flowed through my hands. I knew for sure the Holy Spirit was in this place, as I was being led deeper into prayer.

"Oh, Father: I come before Your throne in the name of Your wonderful Son, Jesus Christ of Nazareth. Father, forgive us all of our sins. Lord, I come and present to You, my grandfather. Your Word says that You are the same yesterday, today, and tomorrow. According to John 14:12, You said that the work that I do, you will do; you shall do even greater works than Me. Lord, I ask You to heal my grandfather of any sicknesses and diseases of any kind, in the name of Jesus Christ. Lord, I ask You now to release Your healing and miracle virtues into his body, in the name of Jesus Christ. Release Your healing and miracle anointings into his body, from the top of his head to the soles of his feet. Heavenly Father, I ask You to make him whole again. I ask You to put a hedge of protection in and around him, this hospital, and this room. I apply the blood of Jesus over his body, from the crown of his head to the soles of his feet. In the name of Jesus, I command his blood cells to destroy every disease, germ, heart failure, and virus that tries to inhabit his body. I command every cell of his body to be normal, in the name of Jesus. I make a demand for his heart and joints to function properly. There will be no pain or swelling in his body. Cause fire to fall like rain, Lord. Fill him with the Holy Spirit, with all the Fruits of the Holy Spirit: Your love, joy, peace, patience, kindness, gentleness, and self-control. Father, I thank You for sending Your Only Son, my Lord and Savior, to the cross to be the sacrificial Lamb for all our sins and sicknesses. I bind up every spirit that is not of You. Lord, send them back to the dry places where they belong, in the name of Jesus, and they shall not return. Lord, I thank You that by the stripes of Jesus, I declare him healed to the heavens. Lord, I also pray that You'll allow this to be used to give You all the glory and praise. I now speak life, prosperity, and healing into his body, in Jesus' name. Amen."

The power of the Lord and His presence weighed heavily upon me. Unable to move, I stayed glued to the ground on my knees, giving praises and thanks to my God, for He's been so good to me. Not knowing when or how it happened, it finally dawned on me that I was back seated in the chair. Not only that, but grandpa had a lot of unfamiliar visitors that stopped by to see what all the commotion was about. Gazing to my left, Doctor Pulaski and one of the other nurses were in awe. They stood in the doorway with their mouths open, staring back and forth from me to where grandpa laid. Wiping the tears from my eyes, I faced them.

The nurse was the first to comment. "I'm so sorry, but I'm so in awe right now. I mean, all these years I've worked here, I've yet to see anything like this before!"

I smiled. "All glory to God!"

"Nurse Marie, did you see what I saw?" Doctor Pulaski inquired.

"Not at all. What was it?"

He turned his attention directly to me. "Raven, I can't believe this. I know I'm not going crazy. Two angels were standing right here in this room while you were praying. One of them was a man. He stood next to your grandfather and rubbed his heart and chest area while the other one—oh my goodness; she was so beautiful—stood hovering over you with her hands folded behind her back. She was standing at attention like in a military-style, but more like a thug. It was like she was there to protect you. Her wings were so bloody, and half of her right wing was missing—like she had been in a fight. Wow! That was very cool of you!"

I couldn't help but giggle a little to myself. "Guys, listen: None of that was me. That was all God Himself, so all glory and honor go to Him."

"God? And this is the same person you kept telling me about earlier, right?"

"Yes."

"You mean to tell me that He's the same person who's going to heal your grandfather…the One I'm unable to see or touch?"

"Yes, that's Him: The Only Living God. He sent His Son Jesus to die on the cross for all of our sins so that we can have a new life."

Doctor Pulaski wasn't convinced. "But I'm a Jew, and the Messiah never came. In fact, I'm still waiting on Him."

"He's already come, and He died so that we can be forgiven. The next time He comes back will be to take us home—the ones who believed in Him."

"But wait; I do believe in God," came the doc's quick response.

"I understand that, but have you accepted His Son Jesus into your life to be Lord over your life?"

"No," both replied in unison

"Listen: Jesus already came and died. He cannot die twice. He's alive right now and seated in Heaven with His Father. Jesus is the Living Water. He said that whoever drinks the water I give them will never thirst again. The water that He gives will become in us a spring of water welling up to eternal life."

"Please tell me more. I want this Living Water for myself. What must I do?" the doctor asked.

"I don't wanna have to ever worry about being thirsty again, so please give me the Living Water," Nurse Marie said.

"It's simple. Jesus said whoever hears His Word and believes that God has sent His Son has eternal life and will not be judged, but has crossed over from death to life."

Both smiled then said, "I want this eternal life that you're talking about!"

"God already had this day ordained. That's why He sent me; to save souls for Him. If you're ready to accept Him, please repeat after me."

Doctor Pulaski and Nurse Marie entered fully into the room and came to stand near me.

"Heavenly Father, I confess that I am a sinner and have sinned against You. I'm asking You to please forgive me. I believe that You sent Your Son Jesus Christ to die on the cross for all my sins. I believe that He died, rose again on the third day, and is alive right now in Heaven. I choose to repent and follow You to be my Lord and Savior, in Jesus' name."

After the duo spoke the last words, the room fell silent.

"That's it!" I said.

"Wow! That's all I had to do to be saved?" Nurse Marie asked.

"Yes. Now, both of you are children of God. That also means we're brothers and sisters in Christ Jesus!"

"Quick question," Doctor Pulaski added. "I've always heard people talking about Heaven and Hell. So, if I die, I'm going to Heaven, right?"

"Not IF you die, but yes: Those who have accepted Jesus go to Heaven WHEN they die. The angels in Heaven are now having a party! They're up there rejoicing! One more thing: Both of you look at me and tell me you are saved."

A praise party immediately broke out in the room.

"I'm saved! Yes, I'm saved! Ohhh, I feel good! I feel so good, so good, so good that I'm saved! Yes, I'm saved!"

"It doesn't stop there, you two."

"Okay," Doctor Pulaski said.

"Now you have to find a church to attend—one that reads and teaches straight from the Holy Bible."

"I don't know of any. Do you have one in mind to suggest?" he asked.

"Actually, yes! I just became a member of this new church I started attending about six months ago. It's really great. Wonderful people are there who will help you as a new believer. As well, it's not too much of a big church. That name of it is Jesus Proclaim Ministry."

"And what type of Bible would you recommend?" asked Nurse Maria.

"I have one of those Life Application Study Bibles. It's easy to read and comprehend."

Both doctor and nurse thanked me for helping direct them to their new lives and walked out of the room with a pep in their step and smiles on their faces—and in their hearts.

While they were walking away, I thought to myself that God sure does have a great sense of humor. It amazes me how He organizes the things He wants to accomplish. He sets them in perfect order, and nothing or no one can stop what He has planned. I smiled again at my Father's work while I watched the duo hopping and skipping down the hallway, trying to shake every hand they met and telling them that they're saved. I am thankful that God has chosen me—a broken vessel—to be a representative of His Son.

On the third day, I walked into the hospital and stood in the hallway with flowers and balloons in tow, listening and watching as the scenery before me unfolded itself. I entered grandpa's room and was greeted by Doctor Pulaski, Nurse Marie, a few of the other nurses, and grandpa himself. He was obviously happy to be alive.

"There's something different about you, grandpa."

"What is it, dear?" he asked.

"You just have this glow. You look much better than before."

I was impressed. Doctor Pulaski told me that when Nurse Marie was doing her regular checks this morning, she found my grandpa watching the television. Doctor Pulaski also mentioned to me that the nurse thought my grandpa was dead. He then showed me the results from the new tests he'd ordered. At first, he thought he was viewing someone else's lab results. He, admittedly, ordered a second series of tests to be done, as he was shocked at the results of the first set. It was a miracle! The second verified the first!

Man says one thing, but it is God who has the final say in one's life. What is impossible with man is always possible with God!

Chapter 26: Raven
No. She. Didn't!

After being confined to the hospital for an additional two days after his miraculous recovery, grandpa was finally released. One of his first questions caught me off guard: "Do you mind if I go with you to church tomorrow?"

"Of course not, grandpa. I wouldn't mind at all." *Oh boy; I'm gonna need to have a conversation with Jesus about this one.* Politely excusing myself from the dinner table, I went to my room, closed the door tightly behind me, and had a moment with my Daddy. "Daddy, I don't know what this is all about. It feels kinda weird to me, but whatever it is that You're doing, I trust You."

Like clockwork, bright and early Sunday morning, we walked through the double-doors of Jesus Proclaim Ministry and sat in the front row. We were jamming as the choir made its grand entrance. I sang along with them. When they were finished, Sister Love began a solo that made the congregation jump to their feet. Grandpa fell on his knees and broke down crying. When Sister Love was through singing, everyone in the church—including me—was drenched in tears.

"The anointing of the Lord is richly in this place this morning," Pastor Demming said, taking his place behind the podium. "I worship You, Lord. Oh, I magnify Your name, Lord. I bless You. I praise You. Come on, somebody; sing along with me and give the Lord His praise! 'Lord, prepare me to be a sanctuary…' Come on, somebody. Whether you know the words or not, give joyful praise unto the Lord, for He is good and His love endures forever! Everyone, continue to stand on your feet and give our God some praise. Give Him what's rightfully due to Him. He woke you up this morning. You have breath in your body because of Him. Some people didn't make it this morning, but YOU found favor with the Lord! He gave YOU another chance! Look at the devil in the eye and say, 'Devil, you are a LIARRRR!' Hallelujah! If God's been good to you, sing your highest praise! Give Him your highest worship!

"Yes, Lord: You're worthy. You're worthy to be praised. We love you, Lord! You're worthy of our praise. Help me praise the Lord! Shout right now! Don't just sit back with your mouth closed. Don't worry about who's looking at you. Don't worry about who's watching or laughing at you. While they're busy looking at you, God is busy looking at them. Somebody look at your neighbor and say, 'Neighbor, don't worry about what they say. There's a breakthrough coming with your name on it!' Say, 'Neighbor, the floodgates of Heaven just released the breakthrough you've been waiting on!'

"Come on, somebody! That same breakthrough you've been waiting on for years has just been released—and your name is written all over it! The devil can't stop your show. What God has for you is for you; no one can take that away. It's all ready for you. No one can steal it! Somebody ought to shout 'HALLELUJAH!' Somebody ought to praise Him like you can't praise Him anymore. Give Him thanks. What an awesome God we serve! He's wonderful! I don't know about you, but I love MY God! I could have been dead a long time ago. The doctor gave my wife the papers to sign because he said there was no more hope for me, but MY GOD! Mmmhmm! MY GOD said, 'Not today! It ain't his time yet! I ain't through with him yet! There's work to be done!'

"Saints, don't let no one write you off and tell you that it's impossible. If God's in it, you better believe it's possible! You don't hear me. I said: As long as JESUS is involved in your plans, your dreams, and your life, it's guaranteed! Say 'Thank You, Jesus! I love You, Lord!' Praise God, saints! Praise Him!

"I wanna talk a little about the importance of the cross, with the main focus on deliverance from guilt," the pastor went on to say. "There's someone in this room right now who God sent me to tell: Let go of the shame and guilt that you're holding on to. He's already forgiven you for those sins. Now, you need to let it go and move on. You know; this had nothing to do with the topic I've been studying to talk about today. For some strange reason, Jesus woke me up this morning quite a bit earlier than normal. He said, 'Robert?' I said, 'Yes, Lord. Is that You?' He said, 'There's someone I want you to tell this morning to release the guilt that they're still holding on to. Tell him to forget the former ways of life and former things. Stop dwelling on the past.' I replied, 'Yes, Lord. Let Your will be done. I'll do as You asked of me.'"

I looked over at grandpa. He was shaking his head and began to shed some tears. Pastor Demming announced altar call, and grandpa obliged. He rededicated his life to Christ and was delivered from lust—a demonic spirit that had kept him bound for years.

God, indeed, had this day appointed. As soon as the service was over, grandpa invited me to have lunch with him. I sat nervously, shaking in my seat as I sat across the table from him. Just as I took my first bite of the pasta I was eating, he opened his mouth and confessed his many sins, seeking forgiveness from me. I nearly dropped the fork when he told me that all along, my mother knew of him molesting and raping me. Actually, it was her idea. When she and daddy first got married, grandpa caught her with a crack pipe and was about to tell daddy her secret when she approached him and made a deal: In exchange for keeping her secret, she would turn her head to him molesting me.

Grandpa didn't want daddy to marry her. In fact, he pleaded with daddy not to follow through with the wedding. That was just the reason daddy needed to file for divorce.

Chapter 27: Kelis
Blessed and Troubled

"Is he dead yet?" I asked.

"Girl! That's the first thing you say when you call somebody phone?"

"Puuleeze! Like I said: Is he dead yet?"

"Is who dead yet?"

"The damn devil."

"You want him gone that bad, Kelis? Why would he be dead, though?"

"I'm just saying. I figured your 'God' would already had done struck him dead."

"Actually, MY GOD healed him. He's very much alive."

"Since when did God start doing business with Lucifer?"

"Girl, have some respect. At the end of the day, he's our elder—and he's still granddaddy, so we must show him respect according to what the Bible says."

I sucked my teeth and replied, "You sounded so dumb just then."

"What's your problem, Kelis? He almost died! You forgot?"

"So, you mean to tell me that God felt that damn sorry for Satan and took the time outta His schedule to heal him? See? That's what I'm talking 'bout. What type of God is that?"

"The loving, forgiving, and caring God. And not only that, but he also got saved."

"OH, HELL NAH! Tell me the name of that church and where it is so that I can stay far away from it 'cause believe me, that church gon be burnt down!"

"Man, your brain's really fried for even thinking like that."

"Raven, I ain't lying. I'm dead serious. I'm guessing your God was high on drugs or drunk on some of that wine He made from water. He changed the water into wine, got lifted, and then allowed that man to walk up into the church house. So, hold on: You mean to tell me that his name is now written in the Book of Life and he gon make it to Heaven?"

"Sure 'nuf!"

"Jesus needs to give me some of what He was smoking 'cause that had to be some good stuff!"

"I'm not gon entertain this mess no more. What you really want 'cause I gotta go finish packing up my stuff?"

"What you packing up for? Where you going, Raven?"

"Oh. My bad. I ain't tell you, but I'm moving away to New York. I was blessed with an academic scholarship for college."

"Oh wow, Sis! I'm happy for you! So, when was you gon share the good news with me? After you left or after you walked across the stage?"

"Girl, chill. I was gonna tell you before I left. I don't know why you jumping down my throat like that. I can never keep up with you."

"Okay, Ms. Big College Girl! At least one of us is doing something productive in life. You the blessed one. Me, on the other hand, gotta do what I gotta do to survive the bricks that are being thrown at me."

"We are all blessed, Kelis. Some are blessed in ways others are not. And girl, only if you knew what it took for me to get to this point. I can tell you this much: By no means was it easy getting there. God has kept me close so that I wouldn't let go."

"Alright, now. Enough with all that. Bye—before you get to catching the Holy Ghost on me and start preaching, speaking in tongues, and all that."

"Yeah, I agree 'cause you'll never understand. I just hope that you do before it's too late."

"Bye, Raven."

"Bye, Sis."

****

"Y'all ready to go get this money?" Zariah asked.

"Hell, yeah!" everyone shouted.

"Zari, drop me off at my lil spot. Y'all already know that you hot, so I don't need y'all coming up in there with me messing up my money."

"Who you supposed to be putting down on, Tamiesha? I don't see no problem with us coming in. We can just come in after you and everyone go their separate ways."

"Girl, I said no. What part don't you get? We can do all that at another store. Y'all can't blend in nowhere. You know damn well they gon remember y'all's faces, so hell no! Just let me go in and get what I need to get, then we can hit up another store and y'all just do you."

"Zari, what you got to say 'bout that 'cause you know damn well that ain't fair," I protested.

"Miesha, that ain't my business. I ain't got nothing to do with that, but she did make a valid point."

"So, you taking sides now?"

"Girl, miss me with that. It ain't 'bout taking sides. It's what makes logical sense. We still got the whole day to make some moves, so just chill and let her have this one. The next stop is on y'all."

By the time I sold all my merchandise, I had counted off three racks I had made to add to my savings. The three of us have been splitting all the bills in the house on our three-bedroom apartment, but all that will soon have to cease. Lately, I've been noticing Zariah acting funny. Suddenly, she wanna make all these off-the-wall house rules, talking 'bout no smoking in the house and how we can't have no guests over after eleven. I'm paying rent. When did I start living in a shelter? I don't know what's gotten into her or what the hell she been inhaling lately, but she got a girl real messed up, and she'll soon find out the next best thing is coming.

"Kelis, before we head out, I need to holla at you for a second."

"Yeah. Wassup? We can talk right now."

"I done asked you a thousand times to stop letting your guests spend the night in my house like they live and pay some bills 'round here."

"YOUR house or OUR house? The last time I checked, Zari, we ALL pay bills in here. How else you think my part of the bills be getting paid?"

Zari put her hand on her hip, and her neck got to snapping. "You know what? It's sad to say, but this ain't gon work. Your mouth is too wild. You have no respect for my crib. My bad, but you gotta go."

"Ain't no pressure. I was gon do that regardless. Just take me with you on this last run and give me a few days to find a place, then I'll be out your way."

At the mall, everyone stayed behind while I went in to handle my business. I wasn't inside the store more than 10 minutes when security approached me and ordered that I go with him to the office in the back.

"What you touching me for? I know how to walk."

"Ma'am, you must come with me. Security is at the door, so there's nowhere for you to run. You might as well come on before things get worse."

I snatched my arm from his grasp. "I promise: If you put your hands on me one more time, I'm gonna empty this whole can of mace in your mouth!"

"Okay, fine. I won't touch you again—as long as you keep walking."

With all the merchandise I had on me, I knew I was about to go down. Curiosity settled in. Boosting is my hobby. I've been doing it for so long and have never gotten caught, so why now? The security officer confirmed my suspicion when he told me that someone called the store and told them to be on the lookout for me.

Hours later, I sat in a cold jail cell getting booked. Since no one paid my bond, I was then transported to the facility where the women were housed.

The people who claimed to be down with me left me for dead. The night I was arrested, I called Zari and asked her to bond me out. Her answer was, "Don't worry; I got you." Two weeks later, I'm still sitting here.

"Girl, you look like it's your first time in here."

"Yep."

"Chile, what they say you did?"

"Stealing."

"Stealing and you STILL sitting in here? I know the judge gave you a bond."

"Yeah, girl. Tell me 'bout it. My so-called homegirls set me up. One of them was supposed to post my bond. I know how that go though: outta sight, outta mind. And that's exactly what they did 'cause I'm still here. It's all good, though."

"Well, my name is Lady. What's yours?"

"Kelis."

"Well, Kelis, I'm getting out tomorrow, and I can put you down with my Daddy."

"Your 'Daddy'? You asking me all these questions like we on trial or something. What the hell you in here for?"

"Violation of my probation and a new charge: grand theft. They hit me with six months, but that's Broward County for you."

"Well, wassup with your Daddy? What he gon do for me?"

"Yeah, about that… How much is your bond?"

"Six beans."

"Girl, that ain't nothing. Ten percent of that ain't nothing but $600.00. Don't worry, though. I got you. When I get out, I'm gon holla at Daddy 'bout bonding you out. And you real pretty, too. Hell yeah! You can definitely make him a lot of money."

"Lady, I make my own money." *Still, I was ready to get outta here. I had to ask:* "So, make him some money doing what?"

"What you think? I know you 'bout that life, so stop acting green."

"Well, wassup? Put me down with your Daddy, then!"

Chapter 28: Kelis
Tramp and the Lady

"**L**ady, let your friend borrow some clothes. Man, she can't be walking 'round here looking like that in them same clothes."

"I'ma take care of her, Daddy. She pretty, ain't she?"

"Yeah. She gon be my new lil PYT." That comment made Lady change her expression from a smile to frown quick—a frown that was also obvious to all the other girls in the house.

"Come on, girl. You know I got you," she said as we went inside her room.

Lady has been Money Mike's girl ever since she arrived as a 17-year-old runaway from Louisiana. She moved to Florida after her stepdaddy—who started raping her at nine years old—turned around and killed her mother when he was confronted with the allegations of the rapes. Lady made Money Mike the most money. On a bad day, she could rake in at least three racks a night. Lady goes hard in the streets. She goes hard at her profession and is loyal to her owner. Her trust landed her the throne as the Madam of the house. Her position came along with great benefits: her own mini-place in the house that sits by itself, a C-Class Benz that Money Mike bought her, and the option to work whenever she liked.

I didn't mind accepting the hand-me-downs Lady was letting me borrow 'cause at this point, the only thing I owned was the dress I wore the first day I entered the house.

"Turn around, girl. Lemme see how you look before we go back out there with Daddy."

"How I look, Chile?"

"Anything my hands touch turns out good. Come on. Let's go 'cause Daddy wanna see you. And don't worry girl; you can be yourself. It's enough of him to go around for all of us."

On the way to Money Mike's room, nervousness settled in. I had no idea what to expect from him. During my two days in the house, I've already heard horrifying stories of how he treats his girls.

Money Mike is a man no one wanna play around with. He has two rules:

1. Don't mess with his money; and
2. Don't mess with his money.

All the other girls who once played around on him either ended up six-feet under or, even worse, were brutally cut up into pieces. The one exception was the last girl, Mariah. She was the only one brave enough to test the waters. Unfortunately, she is still employed by Money Mike…even though she was now missing a leg.

"Hi, Daddy," I said as I walked into his room. His was one of 10 bedrooms in the mansion that sat off by itself on the east wing of the house. His room alone was like a whole house built inside of a castle, with a private entrance that led to a private garage.

"You can relax, Ma. I ain't gon bite you."

"My bad. I ain't know it was that obvious," I replied nervously.

He escorted me to his mini bar where we shared a bottle of liquor. The boost from the alcohol took us to a whole other level. Within minutes, he held my face in the palm of his hands as our lips intertwined. He carefully undressed me, laid me on the bed, got undressed, and laid on top of me.

"Tonight, it's all about you, Ma. I gotta equip you for what's ahead out there. Plus, I like to see what I'm investing in."

Satisfied with his flavor, he said, "It's better than what I was expecting. I'm changing your name to Sweetie." The next two days, the heat was turned up. All the other girls in the house were throwing shade because of all the attention Money Mike was showing me.

My first night on the block, I ended up with a retired Federal judge who had recently lost his wife to breast cancer. He spent two hours telling me about his wife. He claimed her diagnosis was the first time he'd ever thought about stepping outside of his marriage. I told him that technically, she had received a death sentence, so that didn't count. As I listened to him, I sat there staring at him wondering: *Who are you tryna convince? Yourself or me?*

"You know, you're a gorgeous girl. You shouldn't be doing this."

I don't know if it was the alcohol or his recent loss that was doing the talking for him, but I knew it was time to go. I figured he had a set of magnifying eyes that read my mind 'cause I was starting to get bored the second he opened his mouth with that lie.

At the end of my service to him, he handed me an envelope. When I looked inside, I noticed it was stuffed with one-hundred-dollar bills. Already knowing the answer, I asked anyway. "All this for my Daddy?"

"Be smart, my darling. It's all yours."

****

"Hey, Daddy! I'm home!" I said when I walked through the house. I found Money Mike in the game room, one of his favorite parts of the house.

"What you got for Daddy?"

"It's all there, Daddy. Thirty-five."

"Good girl. You just made Daddy proud. You see that it doesn't take a lot to make Daddy proud," he said as he counted off the crisp one-hundred-dollar bills.

Yeah, this 'good girl' ain't no damn fool. Money Mike wanted all his girls to make no less than $1,500.00 a night. He didn't care whether it was a good or bad night. He didn't care how you manage to get it, either. It's been that way since day one; either you deal with it or you leave—but there won't be no one leaving without paying a price.

****

"What makes you think you can be in here laid up in the bed while everyone else gotta be out working the streets for their keeps?" Lady asked.

"Look, Lady: I ain't feeling good, so you better get up outta here before it really be me and you. I ain't in the mood, so you better get out of my face," I snapped.

"And why you ain't feeling good? Who done got you knocked up?"

"Girl, I'm serious. Get the hell out my room."

"You not feeling good ain't got nothing to do with me. You need to get up, get dressed, and go make Daddy some dollars."

"Don't play with me, Lady. I've been working like crazy— non-stop for damn near five months. My whole body is in pain; knees, elbows, ankles, and all. They need a break. Hell, I need a break away from you and your damn Daddy! Both of y'all can go to hell with all that."

"That ain't nothing new. You knew about the repercussions before you took the job."

"Girl, get outta my face! That was then. Past tense. Tell me 'bout today. I don't wanna hear nothing 'bout what you told me way back then. On top of all that, I done had it up to here with you. I'm starting to get tired of all this mess. This type of lifestyle is starting to get to me. Now, all of a sudden, I've been getting this ill feeling. It's like when I'm with my Johns, and I gotta force myself to act as if I'm enjoying myself. Lately, it's been getting even worse. I've noticed that after I'm finished, I get this disgusted feeling."

Lady was unmoved. "I ain't tryna hear your sad story. So, what you wanna do 'cause I can't have you in here like this? When Mike gets back, I gotta give an account of what's what."

"Honestly, I can't go out tonight. I really need some time alone. Please, Lady?"

"Alright. I got your back this time—at least until you feel better. Don't make this a habit."

"Thanks, Lady. I got you."

Chapter 29: Raven
I Choose to Wait On the LORD

Between working a full-time job, classes, and attending church services regularly, things were not as I expected them to be. The little bit of money I had managed to save back home was long gone by the end of my second year.

"You've been sitting in that same spot reading that thing. It's Friday night. Come out with me and let's have some fun!"

"Nah, Hannah: I'm good. I'm gonna pass on that offer and, by the way, this 'thing' that you referred to is called a Bible."

"Come on, Raven; just one time. College is supposed to be fun and, besides, Jesus will understand. I've never heard anyone mention about Him saying y'all people can't have fun."

"You're right. Christians can have fun—just not the type of fun you're referring to."

"UGH! You take this Bible stuff too serious. It ain't like He here with us and sees you. The only way He'll find out is if you open your mouth and snitch on yourself!"

"Girl, I ain't going. God knows everything, so I don't know where you got that theory from."

"OMG, Raven! You're so boring. Well, I guess I'll see you tomorrow, then. Hey, you wanna try some of this? It'll help you stay awake."

"What is that?"

"Nothing that will hurt you. Come on. Just try it with me."

"Lemme see it. Ewww! Why it smell like that?"

Hannah laughed. "I don't know or care about the smell. That's just how it is. Here. Try it. If you close your eyes, you won't smell it that much."

"Nah. I'm straight on that."

"Please, my sister from another mother; just do it with me one time. It'll give you some energy. I promise I won't ask you again, but I know you gon love it! If you try it with me, I'll let you get some of my clothes so you can look cool."

"So, you tryna say that my clothes be looking stale?"

"No. I'm just saying that you can look cool in MY clothes."

"Uh-uh. I'm definitely gonna pass on that, too. I don't wanna look cool. I love being the outcast."

"Sorry, Raven. I didn't mean it like that. If you change your mind, just let me know."

"That's fine with me. I accept your apology—and I won't be changing my mind."

****

"Mamacita, what are you doing?"

"Oh! Hi, Ms. Garcia. I'm just here studying for a test I have on Thursday."

"Mami, you don't worry, okay? You're a very smart girl. You will pass that test with no problem, my friend."

"Aww! Thank you so much, Ms. Garcia, for the words of encouragement!"

"Yes, dear. I wish my daughter was like you. I won't take up any more of your time. You go ahead and continue studying. By the way, Raven, if I ever catch my husband cheating, I will kill him and go to jail. I'll need YOU to be my lawyer."

We joined one another in a good laugh.

"Now, you need to stop, Ms. Garcia, 'cause you know your husband loves you too much to cheat on you."

****

After class was dismissed, I was approached by my financial advisor as I headed towards my room. "Hi, Raven. Can you come with me to my office, please? I would like to speak to you." Once we were settled in her office, she pulled out a file with my name written in bold letters. "I was going through your file this morning and realized that your first payment is due no later than March 8th."

"I'm not understanding your statement. There has to be a mistake of some sort. I was given a full academic scholarship that should have already taken care of all my financial needs."

"As I stated to you during our initial meeting, you weren't awarded a full academic scholarship. After deducting the total costs for your books and tuition, the balance was not enough to cover the costs for your living expenses."

"And how much do I have to pay outta pocket?"

"Let's see. Uhh..." She scanned the file, looking for the answer. "You owe $1,500.00."

"There's no way I can come up with that amount of money in a month. I'm barely making it as it is already."

"Well, we have a few different payment options that might be available to you. You can either apply for financial aid, a grant, or you also have the option to pay outta pocket. Hold on for a quick second, please. I need to verify some information. By the way, you're only able to apply for financial aid with the signature of a parent."

"And why is that?"

"Your age."

"What are you talking about now? I'll be 23 years old in a few months!"

"I understand your concern; however, you have another year before you'll be able to get qualified for financial aid without a parent's signature. That's just the rules that we all must follow. In the meantime, you can choose the option to pay outta pocket."

"I don't think you're comprehending the words that are coming from my mouth. I cannot afford to pay that money. Is it possible you'll be able to grant me an additional month?"

"I'm afraid I can't do that." She was stern in her response, but I could also see the genuine concern on her face.

"Okay. Well, I guess I'll just have to see what I can do. Thank you."

****

"What's wrong with you? Lately, you've been walking 'round here looking all depressed," Hannah said.

"No, not depressed. I do have a lot on my mind right now. It's just so much stuff going on at once. At a time like this, I just have to trust God."

"You know you can talk to me. What seems to be the problem?"

"I wouldn't even know where to begin." I let out an exasperating sigh.

"We have nothing but time. Besides, that's what friends are for, right? Girl, why you sitting there looking at me like that? What did I say wrong now?"

"Friends? Really, Hannah? When did we form that relationship?"

"Girl, stop it. We've been roommates for what? Three years now? You're the longest roommate I've ever had."

"And why is that? Because ain't nobody else got time to be putting up with you and that arrogant attitude you have?"

"I can't help that I'm spoiled."

"Being spoiled is one thing. You, on the other hand, be acting as if you're above everyone else. You need to chill and understand that not everyone was born with a silver spoon in their mouth."

"Ouch! What you mean by that?"

"Basically, everyone ain't able to floss like you. Not all of us were born rich. No worries, though You'll get it someday. I just hope you'll finally wake up one day before life catches up to you and it's too late."

"You know that I hate it when you talk like that. You be making it seem as if I'm about to die. Enough about me. Tell me what's wrong with you."

"You remember me telling you a while back that I got accepted based off a full academic scholarship I was awarded?"

"Okaaaaayyyy. Well, what that have to do with anything?"

"Girl, just listen. Well, how about Mrs. Middleton came up to me and called herself giving me a friendly reminder that my scholarship doesn't cover my living expenses?"

"I'm not getting the reason why she's telling you that."

"For starters, it means I won't be having a place to live if I don't start paying monthly outta-pocket tuition. Not to mention, my first payment is due in one month, and I don't have the first penny to give to these people."

"Well, are you gonna do something about it?"

"What can I do? I've already asked Ms. Garcia for a loan. She doesn't have that type of money just lying around."

"So, what do we do now?" Hannah asked.

"I've already prayed about it and left it in God's hands. He already knows what I need. Plus, I trust Him. I have faith. Whatever His will is, it's going to happen."

"Girl, you kill me with this mess. How the hell you gon sit here talking 'bout you trust someone who doesn't exist? Not to mention putting your faith in something that's not real."

"He's not a 'something.' He's someone, just like you and me. His name is Jesus. He hasn't failed me yet, so why now? Huh? Why would He bring me this far to fail me?"

"You my girl and all, but you're crazy as hell. I think I'm even crazier to be sitting here listening to you while you talk about this wannabe 'God' who can't even save you!"

"You just don't know. He already done did that. What more saving I need? He sent Jesus—His Son—who later died for us and gave us a new life. Girl, it doesn't get any better than that!"

"He might have given you life, but He gave me none. My parents did that. They could have left me for dead. They're the ones who gave me all the life I need. They continue to give it to me freely every day. Look at all I got; all the luxuries I want AND I'm going to one of the best schools in the nation. The car my daddy just bought me for my birthday...girl, please. You sleep. You need to wake up and open your eyes to reality."

"If it wasn't for God, you wouldn't have had all that you have. If it wasn't for His Son, me, you, and your parents wouldn't be here today. God blessed your parents with the finer things in life. All the money your parents have belongs to God and, in turn, they're able to bless you. Who do you think wakes you up each morning?"

"Girl, stop asking me that dumb question when you already know the answer. Duhhh...my alarm clock! That joker be on time, too! As long as I don't forget to set it at night, I'm good to go in the morning."

"That's so incorrect, Hannah. God woke you up. He gave you life when He blew His breath of life into your nostrils. The alarm clock can't do that."

"You actually want me to believe that this 'God' has that much power to do all that?"

"Hannah, you don't have to believe. At the end of the day, I just want you to know the truth."

"I'm not saying that I believe you, but let me ask you this question: If this 'God' is so real, then tell me how we were born. I mean, I know we came from our mommas and all, but how did we come about?"

"See, after God created everything, He decided to make humanity in His image. It's like this: God already knew from the beginning that He was gon have to send Jesus down here to save the world and bring us back to Him. So, therefore, when Jesus ascended back to Heaven, He needed us—humanity—to rule over everything He created. From the beginning, He had a plan. That's when the first human being was formed from dust. Then, God breathed His breath and gave Adam life. After that, the Bible said Adam became a living being."

"Mmhm. I like that. Sounds interesting. So, you be reading this stuff every day and believe it?"

"Of course. I believe every word that's written. These are His words, and there ain't no lies in this book."

"So, now you 'bout to get kicked outta school if you don't come up with this money. You said you already prayed to Him about it and you think He's gonna help you?"

"Hannah, I don't THINK so; I believe He's gonna come through for me. He knows what's best for me. So, even if He doesn't show up and show out for me, I'm still gonna trust and believe in Him."

"Well, if you'd like, I can help you out with the money," Hannah offered.

"What's the catch?"

"I have a close friend that be making runs to Columbia twice a week. I can holla at him for you and then lock you in with us on our next run."

"Girl, please. You and all your illegal activities. I'm good, though. Thanks for looking out, but I'd rather wait on God."

Chapter 30: Raven
Trusting and Believing

"Wassup, stranger? I haven't heard from you in a while," I said as I answered the phone on the second ring.

"Raven, I need you. Where the hell are you?"

"Huh? I can't hear you. Why you whispering?"

"Just tell me where you at," Kelis asked once again, ignoring my question.

"Girl, I'm in New York at school. Where you think I'm at?"

Kelis started talking very fast. "I gotta get away from Money Mike. I'm tired of living like this. Day in and day out, I'm walking the streets and then putting my hard-earned money in his pockets. I asked him the other day if I can leave, and he had the nerve to tell me that no matter where I go, he'll find me. Sis, please: I need your help. They looking for me right now. That's why I'm over here tucked off in this alley. I'm dirty, sweaty, and talking to you. Give me your address. I'm coming up there."

"I don't have no money, so how you gon get here?"

"Don't worry about all that. This whole time, you thought I was being one of his fools. No one knew I was putting my lil stash to the side for a rainy day."

"When you plan on coming and how? Girl, I'm at work."

"I really need your help, Raven. This nigga done sent his peoples for me. He tryna kill me for real. This damn alley stank, smelling like a whole bunch of dead bodies."

I was beginning to hear her sobs. "Can you tell me what happened? Who tryna kill you?"

"Girl, just text me the address. I can't see nothing down here, and I hear a bunch of noises coming from somewhere. Oh goodness…I think someone is coming. I gotta go. Don't forget to text the address."

The call immediately disconnected.

My internal alarm was alerting me, telling me that something terrible was about to happen to my sister. I quickly texted her the address to my job and said a quick prayer for her. I could hear the desperation and sadness trailing from her voice. If my instincts were correct, danger was hot on her trail.

****

"Come here. Let me tell you something. Oh, Raven! What the hell is that smell? Don't tell me that's your feet smelling so awful!"

"Ha-ha! You are so funny. Girl, quit acting like you ain't never smelled them before."

"Nuh-uh. Not smelling THAT bad! That's what you need to be talking to God about. You need to ask Him to cure that SMELL!"

"Ha-ha! You full of jokes today, huh? I'm just getting off work. Been clocking a whole lot of overtime before I gotta face Mrs. Middleton again soon."

"Are you sure God gon come through for you?"

"It's in His control. Whatever the outcome is gonna be, I'm fine with it. I will always keep my faith and trust in Him."

"Well, listen. I see you and Jesus got a special connection going on. I really need a favor."

I shot her a quick look.

"Nothing like that, Raven! You don't have to give me that look like I was about to ask you to borrow some money. But check me out, Sis: I'm about to go with my friend on this run. We supposed to be leaving in another hour or so. He told me that some of his other runners got caught up the other day. Man, that's some hard time I heard they got, and I ain't tryna go to jail. I'm just not built for that. I want you to pray for me. Pray that God don't let us get caught. I just want Him to allow us to go get the product and bring it back with no problems, alright?"

"Alright. I got you. Close your eyes. Let's pray together. Heavenly Father, thank You for this day. Thank You for being such a forgiving and merciful God, a God of second and even third chances. Lord, I wanna thank You for Your love and that we can come to Your throne boldly at any given time to find grace and mercy in times of need. Lord, I come before You and lift my sister, Hannah. I ask that You'll open her eyes and ears and that You give her wisdom, knowledge, and understanding. Guide and lead her in the paths of righteousness for Your namesake. Let Your perfect will be done in her life. Show her the way that she should go. Help her to make the right decisions and that she'll choose to follow You. Lead her, Lord. I thank You for listening to me. To God be the glory. Amen."

"I don't know what the hell all those words meant that you said, but it sounded good. I feel different already. I guess it worked! Thank you, girl. I'll see you when I get back. Oh, by the way, while I'm gone, keep praying for my friend and me. You got that special touch."

****

"How long you gon keep playing these hide-and-go-seek games?"

"Until I know for sure he ain't looking for me anymore."

"Girl, that man probably ain't even thinking 'bout you."

"Trust: You don't know him like I do. I'm the one who ran off on him without saying a word…not you."

"I just can't believe that you let another individual get you all cooped up in a hotel room for two days. And you done threw your phone away like you crazy. How am I supposed to get in contact with you to make sure you good?"

"Just continue doing what you've been doing. I'm not that far from you."

"So, you're never going back to Florida then, right?"

"Hell nah. I want a fresh start. I feel like this right here might be it for now. That's why I made sure to pay someone to drive me all the way up here. I'm ready to start over, Raven. I'm so tired of running. That's all I've been doing all my life 'cause that's all I know how to do."

"I'm sorry, Sis. I understand how you feel and trust this: God knows. He's been patiently waiting for you to come back home to Him. His arms been wide open for the day when you'll make up your mind to let Him take the wheel."

"Raven, I don't know," she managed to say between sobs. "I don't know when all of this started for me."

"You don't, but God does. He also knows when it's gonna end. Girl, you are so special to Him. You're one of His chosen vessels, even though you're broken into pieces right now. Jesus loves you, regardless of your flaws, your past, and the things you've done. He'll never give up on you nor will He ever turn His back on you. No matter what your past is, you can still be used by God."

"How can He love me? How can He love someone like me? I'm such a failure, disappointment, and total mess."

"Girl, don't you know that Jesus already knew everything you was gonna do before you did it? He knew before you even thought about doing it. Do you think my life is perfect? You see what I go through—and I'm a Christian. But that don't mean a thing. I have faults, too. We all do, but God still loves us despite all that. No matter what we do or say, He'll never take His love away. He hasn't left you, Sis. He's with you everywhere you go. You were the one who left Him, and He's patiently waiting for you with His arms open wide, telling you to come back home where you belong."

"Will He be able to forgive me, though? That's the question—even though I've been so angry at Him for all these years."

"Believe me when I say this: You ain't the only one who's been angry at God. There are tons of people who probably feel the same way. The great thing about all of that is HE never changes. God don't hold grudges. He'll forgive you when you go to Him and ask for forgiveness. The only thing left after that is to forgive yourself."

Chapter 31: Raven
Freed from the Grip

"Uh-uh. Why you coming up in here like that while I'm in here using the bathroom?"

"We need to talk."

"Can this wait until I'm finished?"

"Not really. This is urgent, so come on. Get up and let's have a talk."

"Girl, why are you sweating like that? What happened to you?"

"What happened to me? Do you really wanna know what happened to me? Huh? Let's see; everything is wrong. That's what the hell happened."

"Hold up. You need to tone that down a notch and talk to me like you have some sense."

"Well, you remember praying with me, right?"

"Of course." A knowing smile crept across my face.

"Well, on our way back with the stuff in the car, before we got on the turnpike, we stopped to get some food. Once we got back on the road, outta nowhere, I brought up to my friend that me and you had prayed. I shared with him some of the things we had spoken about and how I was kinda interested in learning more. I mean, he been knowing about you being my roommate from the first day you moved in. Then, when I looked over at him, he's sitting there staring at me all crazy like I said something wrong. He looked at me that way for far too long 'cause next thing I know, he ran into the back of another car, lost control of his vehicle, and minutes later, the police were hovering over us like fugitives. We had no way of getting outta the car before they came, so we just sat there. The whole time, all I could think of was you. I don't know how and when it happened, but I managed to get away from all the commotion that was going on. I still can't believe I slipped through the grip of their hands. Honestly, Sis: I can't believe I'm actually alive. With all them police that were there, I'm shocked that I'm standing here having this conversation with you."

She slowed down a bit to catch her breath. That's when I asked, "So, how about your friend? Is he okay?"

"The last time I checked, he was alive and breathing. He'll be getting three meals and a bunk. That fool had the nerve to call my phone talking 'bout why I had to leave him like that? Like we had some Bonnie and Clyde relationship going on."

"Hannah, you don't even realize that God saved you today for a reason. Whatever His reason is, it's up to you to dig deeper to get the answer. Believe it or not, He saved your friend as well."

"Do you actually believe that?"

"Of course, I do. You see: Even though he's locked up, he's alive. Did he get injured at all from the accident?"

"Only a few scratches on his face. That's about it. Nothing life-threatening that I know of."

"God answered your prayer according to HIS will."

"What the hell? We got caught. That's why I told you to ask Him not to let that happen!"

"Your friend got caught. You're here. Besides, even though you guys were doing something wrong, God can still turn his situation around in the blink of an eye and have it be used to give God all the glory and honor."

"I don't see how, when he doesn't even believe in God. I don't even think none of his family does."

"You'll be surprised at what God can do while he's sitting there in that cold jail cell. Jesus can turn an unbeliever into a believer if that's what He wanna do. I've seen an atheist become a believer, so anything is possible with God. Remember: He's the Creator. There's no other God besides Him."

"Oh, yeah. About that. While we're on this topic… Raven, I have something I been wanting to share with you. You remember that one time when you were telling me about Heaven and Hell being real and all that?"

"Yeah. I remember. What about that specifically?"

"Well, I wanna know if you think I'll still make it into Heaven, even though I'm such a horrible person?"

"What you mean by that? Everyone in this world has done some horrible things at one point. Then, when we come to know Jesus, we become a new creation."

"You see, I've never shared this part of my life with anyone. For some strange reason, I feel like I can trust you, so please: don't judge me."

I sat down close to Hannah, began rubbing her shoulder, and looked her square in the eyes. "Go on…"

"I didn't get to where I'm at in life overnight. Before all this came about, I was once a prostitute. I was sold into human trafficking. My parents owed these people some money, and they decided to sell me to pay off their debt. I started being raped when I was seven years old. My tormentors would go days without feeding me, then take turns raping me. This went on for years. One day, I just got tired and came up with an escape plan. I met this lady who was deeply involved in human trafficking. I made a deal with her and managed to escape after two weeks of thorough planning. When I came to this country, I tried to run away, but they found me. They beat me severely, then left me for dead behind a dumpster. A couple found me and took me to the hospital. When I got there, I found out I was three months pregnant. The beating left me with broken ribs and a broken rib cage. I ended up having a miscarriage.

"Virtually every part of my body was shattered into pieces. It took damn near six months before I was able to walk or talk again on my own—not to mention wanting to be touched by a man. I'm still dealing with that this very day. I still have nightmares from the things that happened to me. The couple that found me adopted me. They nursed me back to health. They don't have any children of their own. My adopted mom told me she can't get pregnant, even though they've always wanted a child so bad. When they found me, they did what they had to do to adopt me. They took care of all the necessary documents that were needed so that they could have me as a part of their little family. I was ten years old when that happened.

"Perhaps now you understand why I said they were the ones who gave me life because, at the end of the day, if they hadn't found me, I wouldn't have been here today to share my story with you. I was barely breathing and my pulse was so weak, they thought I was going to die."

"Hannah, you went through so much hurt in your life. Now I truly understand why you feel the way you do. I'm so sorry you had to go through those horrifying tragedies in your life, but I want you to know that you're not alone—and you're not done yet. Now, I realize why…"

"Why what?"

"Why God placed me inside this particular room."

"I'm not understanding what you're tryna say."

"Girl, if only you knew. We have so much in common." Forgetting that we both had classes the next morning, we stayed awake the entire night talking about our pasts and learning more about each other.

"Raven, would God really allow me into Heaven? Like seriously; even though I was once a prostitute? From everything you've taught me, I would really love to go and meet Him one day."

"What you went through in life was not your fault. You were a child. You were forced into that life. Your biological parents were who God chose to be your parents and care for you. They're the ones who were wrong. You're very beautiful, and God loves you no matter what. Once you invite Jesus into your life to be Lord over you and ask Him for forgiveness, you'll be born again, washed in the blood of Jesus Christ, and a new creation in Christ. And, as time progresses, while God is molding and shaping you, you'll be able to forgive everyone who has ever hurt you—and also be forgiven by the ones you've hurt. Jesus doesn't look at your past; He looks at your heart. Jesus didn't come for those who are 'holier than thou'; He came to eat with the sinners—people like you and me. I love you, Hannah."

"Aww; thank you, Raven. I really appreciate that. You're very special to me. I've always wanted a sister, and now, I have one. I love you, too."

Chapter 32: Kelis
Enough is Truly Enough

"How many of us came today to praise the Lord? If you came here today to give the Lord your praise and you ain't afraid, I want you to stand to your feet with me and make some noise! Shout it out loud! Don't just stand there looking at your neighbor 'cause trust me; your neighbor ain't looking at you. As a matter-of-fact, they ain't worried about you. They came here today to get their praise on. Make some noise! Scream your highest praise to the Most High God!"

The house of the Lord was lit today! I stood to my feet as Deacon Hess asked. I clapped my hands while everyone else was running around shouting and dancing. The people were on a high for Jesus!

"Hallelujah! Praise be to God! Amen! You can go ahead and take your seats. Now, if you brought your Bible with you today, I want you to turn with me to the Book of Jonah. When you find it, go ahead and say 'Amen.'" It didn't take too long for all the people to echo their 'Amens.'

Deacon Hess then began. "Now, saints; Jonah was a man of God, one of God's own prophets. Like most of us today, the Lord gave Jonah specific instructions to look for everyone in the city of Nineveh to warn the people, but you know what Jonah did? Again, like most of us here today, he ran from God. I don't know what he was running for. You can run all you want, but you sure can't hide from God! How many of us in here can relate to what I'm talking 'bout? Ha-ha! I didn't expect to get too many hands in the air. At times, God will ask us to do something—whether it is to give someone a message, pray for another, or even to bless a person—but we tend to get so caught up in our ways and pride that we ignore the message and miss the blessings. But we have to remember that God is humble. If we claim to be a Jesus-follower, we, too, must learn to submit and humble ourselves.

"Saints, let me ask you this: How you gonna hide from the Man who brought you into this world? You can't hide 'cause He's gonna find you. Go ahead and run. He's gonna let you run for a little bit, but not for too long. You can run, run, run, and run until you find yourself in a situation where your back is against the wall. The only One you have to cry out to is the same One you've been running from all these years. Then, when He's ready for you and says to you, 'Enough is enough,' you have no choice but to submit and surrender to Him. Let me remind you that the eyes of the Lord are everywhere all the time. We might run from Him and hide (as if He doesn't already know where we're at). The crazy part about it is He already knew that's where you were heading. He allowed you to take that route 'cause He saw what you couldn't see. He saw the roadblocks, the barriers, and the walls. He also knew the precise time we were gonna stop and cry out to Him.

"God gave us all a choice: We can either choose Him or go the other way. He also gave us the answer and told us to choose Him because with Him, there's happiness, blessings, and everlasting life. But what I don't understand is why we wait until it gets to the point where we're down and out. Why wait? Huh? That's the question I tend to ask myself time and time again. God is not going to force Himself on any of us. He's always the perfect gentleman. He doesn't want us to feel as if we're forced to love Him. I'm just gonna be honest with you, saints: Running from God is like running from the police. It doesn't matter if it takes them 20 years; you're gonna get caught. So, in the end, you're basically running from yourself.

"Now, follow along with me for a minute. I promise not to hold you for long. Going back to chapter one, it talks about Jonah running away to a place called Joppa. There, he boarded a ship. Thinking that God had long ago forgotten about him or where he was, he got so comfortable and had the nerve to fall asleep! He was probably laying down snoring and in a deep dream like, 'Yeah. I dodged the bullet.' Now, while he slept, the Lord sent a wind that caused a violent storm. Everyone on the ship was so scared and had no idea what caused the sudden change in the weather. They were to the point where they even cried out to their own false god. Have you ever been in a situation where you found you've been doing something all your life and getting away with it for so long and then BOOM! A sudden and drastic change happened where everything around you seemed outta your control? You don't know what happened. You might've even thought the people you trusted the most were tryna set you up. You get to feeling paranoid, like everywhere you go, someone is watching or following you. Then, again: BOOM! You're caught, and all the walls come tumbling down on you. The pressure is on. Everyone you call family and friends is gone, and the only One you have is the Lord. He's the only One who can save you from getting that jail or prison sentence. He's the only One who can save you from death or disease. I've been there before. As a matter-of-fact, I've been there a thousand times. I've made promises I had no intentions on keeping. I kept running until one day, God said to me, 'My child, enough is enough." And, in response, I said, 'My Lord, I am ready.'

"Jonah didn't know none of what was going on. He was chilling; knocked out getting himself some good rest. Then, the captain of the ship came by and said, 'Hey, man: How you gonna be down here sleeping when we all about to die? You need to get up and call out to your God like we're all doing.' You see, no one except for Jonah knew that the Lord was responsible for the crisis that was taking place—and he wasn't about to tell them, either. That was his decision, until they decided to cast lots. Hey, I don't blame them, either. If I was on that ship and was surely about to die, I wanna know what's up! Who's the reason behind this? Now, after we done reached all the way out here, almost to our destination, all of a sudden there's a storm? I've been checking the weather all week. At no point did the weatherman say anything about a storm."

That last statement caused an instant uproar in the church.

"When the sailors finally cast lots and it fell on Jonah, now he wanna come clean and tell them who he was. No, brother. Why didn't you give us that information from the beginning? Now, go with me to verse 15. The men took Jonah and threw him off the ship. Into the water he went. Scripture goes on to say that the sea immediately grew calm.

"Saints, let me tell you this right now: Make up your mind today to not run from the Lord. You see, when God has a calling on your life and an assignment for you to do, you're the only one He's equipped to handle that task. Better yet, He's been equipping you for that special project, even while you were on the run. He's going to go to extreme measures to get your attention. He's God alone, all by Himself. He's gonna do anything He wanna do to make sure you surrender. Don't get me wrong: He'll give you the ropes to hang yourself. He'll let you run and then run some more. BUT when He gets to the point when He's tired of chasing you…when He's tired of you playing those little hide-and-go-seek games…He'll surely put an end to the chase—the same chase He started. I know what it feels like to be on a wild chase, running until I was weary and tired. I'm saying to all of you: The Lord knows just what it'll take for you to willfully submit. I'm not saying it will, but it might cause some deaths in your family, the loss of a job, failing health, a broken marriage, or even a jail or prison sentence. Yes, it's going to cause some pain and hurts but at some point, you're going to find yourself on your knees crying, pleading, begging, and surrendering.

"Some of you might not agree. You're probably saying to yourself, 'God won't inflict pain on us.' You're absolutely correct! He's not that type of God. He won't be the one inflicting the pain; we'll be the ones causing it. At times, we're very disobedient and, for some, that's what it takes to get our attention. God has no problem allowing us to hit a roadblock. For instance, let's look at the story of Job. God Himself told Satan, 'Go ahead and do what you do best; but on the man himself, you better not touch him. In other words, I don't care what you do, who you kill, or what you steal or destroy; but you can't touch my child. He belongs to me, and you better not kill him.' The Lord allowed Satan to take from Job all his wealth; he lost his children; his livestock died; he even had the breakout of boils that afflicted his entire body—but Satan could NOT kill him. Back then, Job was the greatest man alive. He had a whole lot going for him, and one would have thought Job would have cursed God. No! He stayed true to his faith. He prayed and cried out to God like many of us do when all the walls close in on us. The Word went on to say that the Lord blessed Job abundantly and doubled the portion of what Satan had stolen from him.

"While Jonah was held in captivity in the belly of the big fish, he was in anguish and pain for three days. He couldn't run anymore. He couldn't hide. Who else could save him but the Man up above? At that point, Jonah made up his mind to submit. He said, 'Okay, God. You won. I agree to do it Your way. Can You please save me and get me outta this situation that You have allowed to come up against me?' That's just like us, saints. At some point in our lives, we were once like Jonah—until God had to intervene or we came to that point when we say for ourselves, 'Enough is enough,' and allow God to take control of our lives."

Chapter 33: Raven
Choose Life!

"Hey, ladies," Raven said as we sat eating our meals. "I have a surprise for you all. It's just a short testimony I wanted to share with you. So, y'all know that yesterday, my first payment was due…or else, of course, I wouldn't have had a roof over my head right now. Last night, right after I came home from work and Mrs. Middleton approached me, this time she had an envelope in her hand. After opening it, this is what I found. Look at what God has done for me. Man, I ain't even gonna lie; He really showed out with this one! Fifty-thousand dollars, y'all! Oh my goodness! I'm so happy right now, I don't even know how to act. I'm holding the check in my hand. I know it's real, but I still can't believe it!"

"Oh my goodness, Sis! I'm so happy for you! You deserve it."

"Me, too, Raven. You have worked really hard for this. You kept your faith, and God kept His promises. Wow! This is awesome! Now, in about another year, we will officially be Hannah Santos and Raven Jones PA, ESQ!"

"Come on, y'all. Let's make a toast to the great news," said Hannah.

"Hold up. Not so fast. We have some more news to be celebrating. How about this morning, I saw on the news that Big Mike was found dead?" Those words caused Hannah to give me that 'What you done did now?' stare. "Girl, don't be looking at me like that. I guess someone beat me to it. Better them than me! But it doesn't stop there. I just found a place, so I will be moving there next month for good. I also have a job interview on Monday for a position at a group home, so please pray for me."

"Don't worry about that. Walk by faith. You're covered under the blood of Jesus."

We spent the next two hours making amends, bonding, and crying as we shared with each other more about our pasts. For the first time in my life, I felt peaceful. Moreso, I was shocked to hear about what Hannah endured as a child and what Raven had gone through right under my nose. I finally had the urge to confess to Raven how jealous I was of her while we were growing up.

"Yeah, I can't wait to tell my parents about you guys and share with them the great news. I can just imagine the looks they're gonna have on their faces. I know they're not going to agree with my choices and won't want anything to do with me, but it's my life. I made a decision that I'm both happy and comfortable with. I want to live for Jesus, and as long as He's happy with my decision, that's what matters the most to me."

"Amen to that, Sis. I'm happy for you."

"Alright. Let's make this toast. I want y'all to know that I love y'all from the bottom of my heart. You are definitely my sisters. I couldn't have asked for anything better than this, and I'm thankful that God has allowed us to cross paths and placed us together," said Hannah.

"Well, I want y'all to know that I'll always be here for you. I love you both as well," said Raven.

"And I love you, too," said Kelis. "Let's high-five each other because today, we are closing all doors to our pasts and opening doors to our future—a new life in Christ Jesus, a wonderful future, and great friendships."

~ THE END ~

Discussion Questions

1. Do you agree with Shanece's decision of not sharing with her daughters about her past? If so, why?

2. Have you ever been in a situation like Shanece's when you felt as if keeping your past away from either your spouse and/or children was the best thing to do? If yes, did you eventually reveal the secrets to them? How did they handle it?

3. What could Pastor Curtis Jones have done differently to prevent him from getting arrested and going to prison?

4. If you were Kelis and were being treated unfairly by your other siblings, how would you have dealt with that situation?

5. Have you ever been caught up in a situation such as Raven's? If so, how did you handle it?

6. Do you feel as if Pastor Curtis Jones was aware of what was taking place with his daughters?

7. Do you believe that God was speaking to you through this book?

8. Have you ever been in a situation where you've been running from God? At what point in your life did you surrender to Him?

9. From reading this story, do you feel as if the grandfather sincerely accepted Jesus Christ into his life?

10. Can you relate to any of the characters in this story?

Contact Author Empress

EMPRESS IS AVAILABLE FOR SPEAKING ENGAGEMENTS AND OTHER PUBLIC EVENTS. CONTACT HER VIA EMAIL AT:

BeautifulDiva88@icloud.com

FOLLOW HER ON INSTAGRAM:

E.m.p.r.e.s.s_D.i.a.r.y

Coming Soon From Empress

PRIZED TROPHY

An Urban Novel

Chapter 1

So, I woke up this morning with sex on my mind—only to realize that my man didn't make it home last night. "Tired nigga," I said out loud. I'm tired of him playing these trifling games. He wants his cake and eat it, too, but I got something for him. No wonder I'm always cheating on him. To ease the tension that was building up, I decided to head to the mall for some serious shopping.

Glancing down at my watch, I whispered to myself, "Perfect timing." My favorite sales clerk should be in around this time. As I entered the mall and headed straight towards my favorite store's lady's department, my eyes caught sight of a few head-turners. I continued on.

By the looks of it, I already knew that I had to have the Giuseppe heels that were screaming my name. My phone rang, interrupting my moment of enjoyment. I quickly looked at the caller ID and saw that it was my favorite client: Shaun. He was a Jamaican native from Boca Raton I met a while back. Good sex and great pay kept me at his beck-and-call each time.

"Yeah. Wassup?"

"Waguan babes. Long time mi nuh hear from you."

"Yeah, I just been chillin'. Wassup with you?"

"Suh mi can see yuh later?" he asked. "Mi want sum ah dat good-good tonight," he continued, interrupting my thoughts.

I felt moist between my legs, and a smile crept across my face at the thought of great sex knocking at my door. The thought of getting paid for 20 minutes was the icing on the cake. I quickly finished shopping, paid for my items, and headed to my truck. I was so caught up doing 80 MPH on the freeway and jamming to my favorite artist, I didn't even see the State Trooper. Luckily for me, he was too busy paying attention to someone else and didn't see my truck flying down the 95.

I pulled up to Shaun's house just in time 'cause as I was about to knock, he opened the door. He was dressed with his robe loosely-fitting, and his manhood stared at me in perfect view. Licking his lips, he grabbed my arm and pulled me closer to him, placing passionate kisses on my lips. Shaun spread my legs with one hand and went to working his magic. I slowly eased out of his reach and closed the door behind me.

Taking off my heels, I motioned for him to follow me and, like a dog, he obediently complied. As we made our way to his bedroom, he laid me on the bed and gently began kissing on my neck. For the next hour, he took his time exploring my entire body. He made his way down to my thighs where he then stopped, and we switched positions. Exactly two minutes later, I saw his toes curl and his body began to shake. I continued rocking his boat.

"Babes, you too bad," he said.

"Just hold on. Mi not done yet," I replied as I pushed him down on the bed and took him on a journey for his money.

See, Shaun is my favorite client. His sex-game is on point; plus, he's always extra generous. We've been messing around for a little over a year. I know exactly what he likes, how to please him, and the right techniques to use. I'm good at what I do. That's what kept me in the game for so long—and I've never had any complaints from any of my clients.

One thing I've learned about this part of the game is to never spend the night with a client 'cause that's how feelings start working their way in. Next comes "I love you." I play my cards well 'cause that's one mistake I'll never make. My feelings are always kept under my feet.

Thinking about my next move, I sat up in the bed while watching Shaun as he slept. I'm sure he was dreaming about what he wished he had for himself. I'll never forget the day I showed up at his house for our normal excitement, only to find him on one knee and a ring in one hand.

I slowly gathered my belongings, collected my coins, and, as usual, made sure to visit his safe. I grabbed a few bonuses, put them in my purse, then made my exit out the same door I entered.

***What does the future hold for this sexually-driven
Jamaican queen?
Stay tuned for details on Empress' future projects!***

www.ingramcontent.com/pod-product-compliance
Lightning Source LLC
Chambersburg PA
CBHW070959180726
48291CB00004B/1361